locked

RECKLESS MC OPEY TEXAS CHAPTER

WALL STREET JOURNAL & USA TODAY BESTSELLING AUTHOR

KB WINTERS

Copyright and Disclaimer

This book is a work of fiction. The names, characters, places and incidents are products of the writer's imagination and have been used fictitiously and are not to be construed as real. Any resemblance to persons, living or dead, actual events, locales or organizations is entirely coincidental.

Copyright © 2019 Book Boyfriends Publishing

All rights reserved. No part of this publication may be reproduced, stored in or introduced into a retrieval system, or transmitted, in any form, or by any means (electronic, mechanical, photocopying, recording, or otherwise) without the prior written permission of the copyright owner. The author acknowledges the trademarked status and trademark owners of various products referenced in this work of fiction, which have been used without permission. The publication/use of the trademarks is not authorized, associated with, or sponsored by the trademark owners.

Table of Contents

Copyright and Disclaimer ii

Chapter One 7

Chapter Two 21

Chapter Three 37

Chapter Four 51

Chapter Five 59

Chapter Six 65

Chapter Seven 73

Chapter Eight 79

Chapter Nine 87

Chapter Ten 93

Chapter Eleven 105

Chapter Twelve 119

Chapter Thirteen 141

Chapter Fourteen 155

Chapter Fifteen 163

Chapter Sixteen 175

Chapter Seventeen	185
Chapter Eighteen	195
Chapter Nineteen	217
Chapter Twenty	231
Chapter Twenty-One	261
Chapter Twenty-Two	283
Chapter Twenty-Three	291
Chapter Twenty-Four	299
Chapter Twenty-Five	309
Chapter Twenty-Six	319
Chapter Twenty-Seven	325
Chapter Twenty-Eight	333
Chapter Twenty-Nine	345
Chapter Thirty	353
Epilogue	363

LOCKED

Reckless MC Opey Texas Chapter Book 3

By Wall Street Journal & USA Today Bestselling Author

KB Winters

Chapter One

Holden

Not this shit again.

That was the main thought running through my mind as the Reckless Bastards gathered inside the Sin Room for another MC church. Another robbery in Opey? We just kicked the ass of those last motherfuckers who tore up the town. I signed on here as a rancher, not a goddamn crime buster.

And why the hell did they call it church? I didn't see any crosses in here. So, it didn't take a damn genius to figure out what had Gunnar's blood pressure on the rise. A slow stroll through Opey proper and you'd figure it out. Hell, a stop for coffee, screws, or an ice-cold beer would get you all the information you needed about the crime spree in town.

Another goddamn crime spree.

At least the latest attack on good citizens of our town hadn't involved any violence. *Yet.*

Which brought us to the reason for the current church meeting. What the fuck were we going to do about it this time?

Gunnar strode to the head of the table and sent his dark scowl around the room.

"Is everyone present and accounted for?"

I felt sorry for any Reckless Bastard who might've decided to skip this early morning meeting.

"Everyone's here," Wheeler, the club's VP said with a sleepy groan. "Church called to order," he mumbled, eyes barely open, probably from a late night with some hot chick.

Gunnar nodded, his gaze settled on each and every one of us just to make sure he had our undivided attention. He did.

"This shit has got to stop," he said. "Some fuckers thinking Opey's their own personal ATM and they can come in here for a withdrawal any time they want."

LOCKED

"Fuck," Cruz said. "Who is this time?"

"B&B," was all Gunnar said. It was all he needed to say. A chorus of curses went up so loud an outsider might have mistaken our meeting for an actual church service.

"Not our twins," Saint snort-laughed.

The beloved but raunchy aging twin sisters ran a bed and breakfast in town. Not to be confused with the young, bitter, tight-ass twins belonging to Martha, our cook, housekeeper, and overall mother superior of our bedraggled troop of misfits. How those two witches came from that woman was one of the great mysteries of the universe. However, our favorite twins, the Monroe sisters, were our concern this morning.

"What are going to do about it?" Saint asked, still wired from last night's shift at the bar.

"Probably shouldn't have left blondie alive," Cruz added with more than a little bit of annoyance. He'd been the one tasked with watching the kid Slayer and Saint brought back from the bar downtown. Slayer actually took out his brother, but Gunnar decided to let the fuckwad go free to send word that Opey belonged to us. Was protected by the Reckless Bastards.

"Probably not, but the shit is done, and we have a different problem now," he shot back, rightly pissed off and knowing Cruz was right. "Nobody's been hurt. Yet. But we all know that shit is just a matter of time."

"You sure this time it's a different problem?" asked Cruz, close to belligerent right now. "Not the same assholes back for another round?"

A quick look around the room proved more of the club was with him than not.

I stood slowly, unfolding my big body from the large table that somehow was still too fucking small for me. I stared at Gunnar.

"We can't know for sure if this is new shit or the same shit," I told him. I agreed with Cruz. We should have offed that blond motherfucker when we had the chance. But as the Prez, it was Gunnar's call to make, which meant he was right, we'd have to deal with the most pressing problem. Who broke into the Monroe's?

Gunnar answered. "Until we have proof it's related to the old shit and the same club is behind it, I say we treat it like new shit."

Saint groaned, and Slayer joined in. "Does this mean more late nights driving around Opey keeping an eye out for bad guys?"

The room erupted in nervous laughter at the prospect of cruising around the world's most boring small town late at night. You couldn't find a burger or even a half-decent cup of coffee past midnight.

Unless you went to our club, The Barn Door, available by invitation and membership only.

Gunnar nodded and raked a hand over his short crop of hair. "Yeah. It does. We need to catch these fuckers, at least one, if for no other reason than to identify them. Once we know where the threat is coming from, we'll be ready to end it."

Wheeler stood and said what we were all thinking. "Are a bunch of petty burglaries really worth our time? Or our wrath?"

The MC had already been through too much shit since its formation, and though Gunnar was confident in our abilities, we had more shit to think about now. It wasn't just us, just a bunch of beaten and battered vets looking for a place to belong in this fucked up world. No, now it was families as well.

Gunnar smacked his fist against the table, drowning out words of agreement coming from around the room with one angry glare.

"We're here now. And Opey is our town to protect. It's our job to keep it safe. Opey has opened up its arms to our MC, our members' club, The Barn Door, and even the police and Mayor are on our side. We don't want to fuck that up."

It seemed a bit melodramatic to me, but Gunnar's grave expression said he believed it with all his heart.

If he believed it, then I believed him. I raised a finger to get his attention. "So we have to find these guys. And then what?"

"We'll figure that out when the time comes."

Gunnar was turning out to be an excellent leader, but he wasn't one for much advanced planning. That didn't sit right with me. Growing up in Opey and living on a ranch most of my life before joining the military, plans were a way of life around here. You had to plan the pasture for the cattle, the crops you intended to grow for the new season. Whether it was harvesting, canning, vaccinations, and even meals, you thought everything out, so life ran like the perfect machine.

Gunnar's approach would take some getting used to.

"Problem, Holden?"

Gunnar was in a mood, and I understood. I'd be in a mood, too, if I had to leave the bed of a warm woman to deal with this shit.

"Yeah. This lack of planning shit is why we're in this trouble now. Let's say we find a pair of burglars tonight. Are we just taking photos? Grabbing one of them? Both of them? Where are we taking them? Because I gotta tell ya, another middle of the night run with a fuckin' body in the trunk ain't my idea of a good night."

It was a necessary move that last time, burying the dead brother in the desert between Opey and Mexico, but not one I was eager to repeat. Hell, I was a rancher, not a fuckin' criminal.

Gunnar looked around the room, seeing half a dozen heads nodding in agreement. He waited a beat, then sighed heavily. "Fine. We find them tonight, we grab them. All of 'em."

"All right!" Wheeler clapped his hands eagerly and smiled around the table. "Saint and Slayer had the magic touch last time, so let's have them take the first shift. Right?"

LOCKED

"Fine by me," Slayer added and smacked Saint on the back. "We made a good team, and it's nice to see the quiet one get fired up."

Saint flipped him off, drawing laughter from the rest of the room, because when we weren't running a sex club or dealing with our demons or keeping our little pocket of Texas safe, we were, at heart, a bunch of silly teenage boys. The only difference? Our scars weren't just on the outside.

"Good," Gunnar said, his deep growl slicing through the muted conversations and laughter around the room. "Holden will take over for Saint at the club. Dismissed." He lifted the metal-studded gavel and smacked it right over Lady Mayhem's face, engraved in the table. Then he issued an order. "Holden. A minute."

"Oooh, Mah-Dick is in trouble," Cruz teased, using the nickname I hated, given to me because of all the heat I packed behind my zipper.

I flipped Cruz off and stayed standing while the room emptied until it was just me and Gunnar left. And his perma-scowl. "What's up?"

"What's your fucking problem?" Gunnar worked hard to be intimidating, and he could be a scary motherfucker. But I grew up on a ranch and then went straight to the US army, which meant I didn't scare or intimidate easily.

"My problem is that you want us to risk our lives, but you don't have a fucking plan, man. Wasn't the shit last month enough?"

He didn't look moved at all as he dropped down in his seat at the head of the table. "That's what we do, Holden. I thought you understood."

"I do. But you have to keep earning that trust we all give you, man. You can't go off half-cocked 'cause you're pissed off. What if something happens to Saint tonight? What will you tell Hazel? Hell, how will you be able to live with yourself knowing you didn't do all you could to keep your men safe? What if you fucking end up in jail?"

"What do you suggest? That we do nothing? 'Cause we tried that shit, and it backfired in spectacular fashion," Gunnar boomed.

LOCKED

"Dammit, Gunnar, you know that's not what I'm sayin'. What do you hope to gain if we find these assholes tonight because you haven't even said where they should be taken? Back on the property? Someplace else?" I let out a deep breath and dropped down in my seat. "I'm with you Gunnar, and I support you, but this ain't your old club. We don't have that history. Half of us don't even know what the fuck we're doing. You have to think and plan like a leader. Whatever happens to any of us will fall on your shoulders. It's a heavy burden, one I don't wish on my worst enemy. Never mind a friend."

He mulled my words over for a few minutes, nodding absently as he collected his thoughts. "You're right. Shit, you're right. I need to do better. And I will. Thanks."

I flashed a slow grin, the one Wheeler called my Cowboy Smile and stood again. "Does this mean you'll find someone else to replace Saint?"

I didn't have a problem with The Barn Door, but the club wasn't my scene, and I didn't like being there.

"Nah. Watching your big ass cowboy body move through the crowds like they're contagious and search for a way to turn down all those horny bitches is way too amusing. On the plus side, we'll be working together tonight."

He stood and clapped me on the back like *that* was a good thing.

"Great, so I'll be covering the whole damn place while you steal off with Peaches for an hour or two?"

"Nah, I know how much you hate working The Barn Door, so I'll just make it an hour."

"Gee, how generous of you, Boss."

Gunnar barked out a laugh. He made his way to the door, and I followed. "Hey, we're trying to make a baby, and it takes plenty of practice."

My laugh trailed behind Gunnar as he climbed the stairs to the top level of the club. "If you need that much practice, you're doin' it wrong. I got some pointers if you want."

LOCKED

Gunnar laughed again as he locked up the doors, turning to smile up at the sun-streaked sky. "My woman has no complaints."

"That you've heard," I mumbled, making him laugh as we hopped on the last available four-wheelers and headed to our separate quarters. I had a few hours to myself to handle chores on the ranch before my shift later, which meant I had time for a few fortifying beers before I clocked in.

KB WINTERS

Chapter Two

Aspen

Date night. It was something every woman looked forward to, especially when their date was a gorgeous blond who drove a BMW the same color blue as her eyes. At least that was how I used to feel about Ken. We'd been dating for about a year now, but lately, things like getting ready for date night felt more dutiful than fun.

Tonight, for example, I'd be more than happy to Netflix and Chill. What the hell was so wrong with having a night in once in a while, anyway? Sometimes a girl just needed to put on sexy lingerie under a pair of yoga pants and a loose t-shirt, just in case there was more *chill* than *Netflix* going on.

But Ken had other plans.

The Barn Door. Though we were in the heart of Texas, complete with cowboys, saloons, and people who tipped their hats at me and called me ma'am, this was no line dancing bar. Nope, it was a sex club.

My boyfriend wanted to take me to a sex club instead of staying home for guaranteed good-time sex. If that wasn't a sign that something was wrong in our relationship, then I didn't know what was.

But with that thought lingering in the back of my head, I dressed carefully for our date. If our problems were sex-related, then the right outfit and a little bit of public fun would turn things right around. I hoped so, anyway. Which is why I opted for the tiniest pair of lace, high-cut red panties I could find. They showed off an ass that was the result of regular Pilates and kickboxing. The matching bra made my tits look big and high and perky, just the way Ken liked them. Now the question was, did I wear something sexy but demure on the outside or just go all out sex kitten?

In the end, I chose a black lace peekaboo dress that showed more skin than it covered because I didn't want to hear Ken bitching about me dressing like a school teacher. Last I checked, teachers didn't wear lace dresses, but *he* was the expert.

"Babe?" The front door of our apartment opened a second before Ken's voice sounded, calling out to me like I was his little housewife.

As if.

"In here!"

I loved Ken, at least I was pretty sure I did, but we were definitely going through a rut. A big fucking rut about as wide and as deep as the great state of Texas. Maybe this Barn Door place would help. Not that it mattered because there was no fucking way on God's green earth I was letting him go to that place alone. He'd get lost in the sea of pussy and might not emerge for days.

Maybe weeks.

He walked into the bedroom, and his gaze immediately lasered in on my tits, which were almost complete cleavage thanks to the push-up bra.

"Damn Aspen, you look hot as fuck. How about a quick BJ before we head out?"

Wasn't that just fuckin' romantic?

"How about a quick sixty-nine instead?"

We *were* going to a sex club after all, and maybe that was what we needed, to be primed and horny when we got there. If nothing else, I'd be relaxed, but that wouldn't happen because Ken had one fatal flaw. He had an aversion to oral sex, giving it, not receiving. Clearly.

"Ah, babe." He rubbed the back of his hand, a tell when he was lying, and flashed his most charming grin, the one that had reeled me right in that night at The Dirty Spur. "But you're all dressed and ready to go."

"But you're okay with messing up my makeup which took me longer to put on than the whole damn outfit?"

Now it was my turn to smile my best Miss Texas *bless-your-poor-stupid-heart* smile in his direction, licking my lips just in case he forgot that he was lucky to have me.

"I guess not." His shoulders slumped as he pushed off the wall, the posture of a spoiled child being told no. "You ready to go?"

Hell, no, I wasn't ready, but it was too late to back out. "Yep. Let's go," my tone more upbeat than I felt. But what good would it do me to get all sullen at the start of our big night out?

We drove over in silence. We didn't even play music. Well, not on the radio. Ken's fingers, however, tapped a quick two-step on the steering wheel nonstop. For miles.

"Ken, what's wrong?"

"What do you mean, babe? Everything's fine." He shot me a distracted smile. It worried me, but I was more relieved that his late nights without me weren't because of another woman.

"You're tapping your hands like you're a nervous wreck. Is everything all right?" As soon as the question was out, his hands stopped, and he gripped the wheel hard enough to whiten his knuckles.

He turned back to me with a wide, sweet smile. It was the smile that made me say yes to a second date, equal parts charming and earnest. "You're the best, babe," he said. "You know that? Thanks for asking about my day."

"Of course. So?"

Ken was always vague about his work, but we lived in a nice apartment. I didn't have to dip into my trust fund to pay for it, which was probably the only reason my daddy hadn't strung him up by his ankles yet. Ken worked from home, taking business calls at all hours. Some days I thought maybe he was a lawyer or accountant for the mob, but Ken wasn't that kind of man. He was more J. Crew than henchmen, but sometimes…I wondered.

"Just some bullshit at work. Nothing for you to worry your pretty little head about." His grin was condescending, but I let him get away with it for now because it was easier than fighting.

And then going inside a sex club. That was a recipe for bad decisions and deep regrets. "If you say so."

"I do, babe." He reached out and ran his thumb along the line of my jaw in what was supposed to be a soothing gesture, but it just made me feel like a child.

I jerked out of his touch and turned to face him. It was time for *the talk* before we got to the club. "We should set some boundaries for tonight."

He gave me some serious side-eye and laughed. "Boundaries? Babe, we're going to a sex club. The whole point is *no* boundaries."

I wasn't even surprised at his response. Annoyed for sure, but not surprised. "So you're all right with me taking two guys at once even if neither of them is you?"

"You wouldn't do that, Aspen. You never even let me in your back door." He licked his lips and ground his hips with a groan. "No matter how much I beg."

"I already told you I would."

He snorted. Derisively. "Yeah, if I lick your pussy. You know I don't do that."

"And you know that I do."

It was an argument we'd been having since our fourth date. I'd given him a world-class blow job, the kind that makes a man do that nervous laughter thing uncontrollably, and he'd slipped inside of me and come in two minutes.

"So…what I'm hearing is that you'll do what you want and I'll do the same?" I said.

I didn't want to have sex with another man, but maybe that was what this relationship needed. Maybe it was the reminder I needed to figure out what to do and where to go next.

"What I'm saying is we should both do what feels right." He gave me a smug grin that almost made my skin crawl.

He'd probably try to push me into some girl on girl action for his viewing pleasure. I wasn't opposed to having a little fun with another woman. I experimented in college, just like everybody else, but it was the pressure I objected to. Some days I dreamed about leaving him for a woman just to piss him off.

"Good," I said, ending *the talk*. "I think so, too."

In fact, the more I thought about it, the more that sounded like an excellent idea.

***

The Barn Door wasn't so bad. It didn't look like a sex dungeon or any weird shit, well if you didn't include all the people in various states of undress. I was probably overdressed given all the women bouncing around in nothing but lingerie, mostly leather and lace. A few brave women wore a combination of both, giving off the perfect Madonna-whore vibe.

The music was loud, pulsing, throbbing. Sexy as hell, in fact. The lighting was dim enough to lower my inhibitions without being creepy or making me feel unsafe. Actually, it was kind of fancy.

So far, I wasn't regretting the decision to check out The Barn Door, then again Ken left to go to the bathroom as soon as we got here. I knew public restroom lines could be insane, but this was ridiculous.

But I refused to be one of those girlfriends. Not tonight, damn him. So I strolled over to the long wooden bar up front because it had beautiful brass embellishments and a big burly bartender who looked like he wouldn't take any shit. That was exactly who I wanted nearby in case any of these horny men got the wrong idea.

Five minutes later, I managed to slide up to the bar. And waited. And waited. The petite, dark-haired woman laughed and bantered while she mixed drinks for a middle-aged foursome. The big burly guy had his head down as he pulled a handle on a draft.

"What can I get ya?" he asked, his voice deep and alluring with a touch of gruff.

"I'll have a cosmopolitan and a Jameson, neat."

LOCKED

A smart woman would make Ken get his own damn drink for leaving me alone like this.

"A Cosmo," he grumbled and looked up with a smile that was more of a grimace as he handed two beers to a young couple. "Of course. Comin' right up."

The good looking ones were always assholes, and I already had one of those, but there was something about the big man that wasn't just appealing. He was familiar. Vaguely familiar, like maybe we crossed paths at a bar or coffee shop.

He was tall, well over six feet with broad shoulders that tapered down to a very slim waist. Even though his chambray was half un-tucked, the big man moved like he was well-built, like he used his body to earn a living. An athlete maybe, though in these parts it was more likely he was a cowboy.

I gave up cowboys a long time ago, yet in a strange twist of irony, ended up a stone's throw away from hometown. "What's wrong with a Cosmo?"

Still, he didn't look up, just mixed the drinks and slid them across the bar.

"Nothin' at all. Cash or tab?"

It took a moment for his words to register, and even when they did, I didn't understand. "Excuse me?"

"Are you paying cash or putting it on your member's tab?" His tone was annoyed and when I looked up, and up, and up, it was into a pair of dark, sapphire blue eyes that looked more than a little familiar. Especially when they were filled with intense emotion like they were now. His nostrils flared. "Well?"

"Um, cash, I guess." I didn't even know if Ken had a membership here. I wondered how he got us in here in the first place.

My dress contained one little pocket that was just big enough for ID and three fifty-dollar bills. Not even lip gloss. "Just a second."

"Hazel. Cash." That was it, just two barked words, and he walked to the other end of the bar, leaving the brunette to finish my transaction.

LOCKED

"Sorry about that."

The girl named Hazel said, "No worries. A dress that gorgeous shouldn't have to deal with messy lines." She winked and quickly made change, leaning in close as she handed me the change. "First timer? Take one big sip and then start walking around. Every time you feel overwhelmed, take another sip until you relax. You don't have to join, just watch the action around you. And have fun." She smiled and turned to take care of the next customer.

I thought about what the woman the big guy called Hazel said as I headed in the direction of our booth with two drinks in my hands, at the mercy of every set of hands kind enough, and horny enough, to offer assistance. Maybe she was right. I should take a look around.

Stopping and changing directions wasn't easy with the crush of people inside the main room, luckily there were mostly naked men and women dancing in human-sized bird cages above. It was a nice distraction. So was Ken's Jameson, which I sucked down quickly and left the glass on the first flat surface I found.

One sip down, at least four more to go.

I found a stairwell between the front room and the back room, which seemed to be even more crowded. And loud. So I opted for the staircase, finding a near-exact replica of a horror movie dungeon.

"Not creepy, sexy," I tried to remind myself and took a sip of my Cosmo.

Inside the first room, I saw a man with two women. One rode his face while the other rode his cock, and even though I couldn't see his face, his hands said he was a happy man. They searched and touched, pinched, caressed and squeezed, eager to touch any of the soft flesh at his access. The women had their heads tossed back in ecstasy, eagerly taking their pleasure from the man.

This was hot, but I wasn't sure I could have sex with someone while strangers watched.

LOCKED

The next room was a mix of couples and groups, draped across jewel-toned cushions. Some kissed and touched like teenagers. One girl was backed into a corner with both legs tossed over wide, dark brown shoulders, a man's head moving to the rhythm of pleasure. A bigger woman was licking a cock like it was her favorite flavor of ice cream while a buff Hispanic-looking man licked her asshole.

My own asshole twitched at that, and I wondered what it would feel like. I stared for a few minutes and found Hazel was right. Even just watching was a thrill. I moved on to the next room, where I got my first surprise of the evening.

There was Ken, shoving his cock into a redhead dressed like a cheerleader, bent over a leather stool while a petite blonde knelt behind him, sliding her tongue in and out of his asshole.

Again, I wasn't surprised. I was annoyed but not surprised.

Stepping inside the small dark room that smelled like sex, sweat, and a blend of perfumes, I let out a deep

35

breath. "Wow, that must have been a really long line in the bathroom."

Ken froze at the sound of my voice but made no move to slide out of the pussy. Or away from the tongue licking him to an ass-gasm. "Aspen, babe. No boundaries, remember?"

No boundaries. "Fuck you, Ken."

"Aw, babe. Don't be like that. It's just a little fun."

A little fun sounded like exactly what I needed right now, and I smiled. "You're right, Ken. No boundaries." I turned away from him, proud of myself for leaving without causing a scene.

And I went in search of my own fun for the night.

Chapter Three

Holden

"You know Holden, this whole brooding cowboy thing only works in romance novels. And movies featuring Meryl Streep." Hazel had the nerve to reach up and pat my jaw gently, before laughing right in my face.

"I'm not brooding. I'm just bein' me."

That much was true. I wasn't a bartender by trade or by passion because I would never—if given a choice—choose to deal with people. Animals, they were much easier than people. Hell, weapons were easier, too.

"I know, and you're great, but maybe a little *less* brooding and bit *more* sexy cowboy with a twang. Yes, ma'am and all that shit, yeah?"

My frown deepened. "You're lucky I like you."

She flashed a saucy grin that was underscored by the blush that stained her cheeks. "I like you too,

Holden. That's why I'm asking you to stop scaring away the customers."

"I'm not," I insisted. Sure, I didn't want to be here, wanted to be anywhere but here, but I gave Gunnar my word that I'd show up and work my shift. Plus, Saint asked me to keep an eye on his woman. Of course, I said yeah, so here I was, helping out, reluctantly, though.

"You are. Men buy the drinks, and you're scaring them off, which means you're fucking with my tips." Hazel put her hands on her hips and let her smile fade just enough to let me know she was serious.

"Okay, fine. Sorry about the mix-up, ma'am." I tipped an imaginary hat her way, and she laughed.

"Perfect. More of that. Thanks."

"Sure." It would've been easier to wear a smile if I hadn't been smacked with a blast from my fuckin' past in the form of Aspen Holt. She was still blonde and still as beautiful as I remembered her. Blue eyes still as pale as the perfect cloudless sky. She'd aged a bit, hell we all had, but she looked good. Better than good.

LOCKED

She was my dream girl all through junior high and high school and totally out of my fucking league. I didn't realize at the time how much money mattered in the world. Her daddy owned one of the biggest spreads in all of Texas and the biggest cattle ranch by a mile in the small town of Vance, not a hundred miles east of Opey. Compared to my family's thirty cattle operation, they were royalty. But with the naivete and bravado of the young, I didn't let any of that sway me. I wanted Aspen, and I convinced myself she'd want me too if she gave me a shot.

What a stupid fucking kid I'd been. Eighteen with more cock than intelligence, I strolled up to her right after graduation. I smiled with my chest all puffed out as I asked her out. She and her friends laughed in my face. *"Not even if we were the last two people on earth, Holden!"*

Bitch.

I reached up for the good tequila and poured a shot, pounding it quickly to wash away the memory of her laughing, cruel face. She was the reason I'd left

Vance and never looked back, not even after I lost everything in the military. Instead, I came to Opey, worked a few ranches, and built a new life here.

Away from her.

Yet, here she was. I downed another shot of tequila and smacked my lips as the liquid burned its way down. Aspen fucking Holt was here. In Opey.

A hundred bucks said she was with some rich fuckin' douchebag who treated her like shit. She'd favored the type in high school and probably still did.

Not that I gave a damn, because I didn't. I was just shocked at seeing her.

Another shot down, and it burned a little less than the last one.

The next time I looked up, my gaze found Aspen at the top of the stairs, looking gorgeous and pissed off and determined. Pale blue eyes scanned inside both rooms, trying to decide where to exact her revenge would be my guess. It happened a lot inside the walls of The Barn Door. Women who weren't wired for this

LOCKED

kind of sexual deviancy convinced themselves they were. She probably found her douchebag with another woman, maybe more than one, and now was in search of her own bad decision.

It was a recipe for disaster. I picked up the phone to call Ford, our handler. "Possible screeching owl situation," I told him, using our code for this exact problem. "Stacked blonde in a tight, black lacy thing."

Having done my good deed for the day, I rewarded myself with another shot of tequila.

***

Dreams were a motherfucker, and I envied men like Wheeler who could lay their head on a pillow and fall into a dreamless sleep that didn't contain the memories of ghosts.

Tonight that ghost came in the form of Ria Santos, a gorgeous Army medic with honey brown skin and dancing hazel eyes. We met on my second tour when I took a bullet to the side. She'd arrived with the chopper to dress me and get me to a nearby care facility. Her dimpled smile had knocked me on my ass, and then she'd given me shit about getting shot.

"You're supposed to duck," she told me with a laugh, shaking her head with a rueful smile.

"Yeah, I did. Just wasn't quick enough, I suppose."

She laughed as if I'd just told the funniest joke around and *bam*! I was hooked. We spent every free moment we could find together. We took leave together, visiting parts of Europe doing the tourist thing. I even met her old man on a trip to Barcelona. He didn't hold it against her—or me—for choosing the Army instead of his Navy, and I didn't hold it against him that he was a Giants fan.

Every night, memories of Ria and our time together came to me, flashed like little snapshots of the short time we had together. Usually, the exhaustion of a long day on the ranch meant I was fast asleep before any more of our relationship could play out. But it turned out that too many shots of tequila and eight hours of tending bar weren't quite the equivalent of ranch work.

And it all came back to me. Not just the good parts, where we were laughing and exploring some ancient city, kissing in front of world-famous monuments, or even better, sneaking kisses when we were on duty, out of view of any superior officers. Of course. No, thanks to the tequila and very likely the appearance of *someone from my past,* I remembered that fucking day like it was yesterday. To me, every damn day was *that* day.

We were on a routine security sweep of the area. All intel indicated there were no un-friendlies in the area. We were out to make sure it stayed that way. Like men tend to do, we were bullshitting. The guys were giving me shit about my not-so-secret relationship with Ria, mocking Jones for being pussy-whipped over his beauty pageant wife and razzing the two single guys for being in serious relationships with their left or right hands.

It was dumb guy shit, a way to pass the time while we were in a literal and figurative hell. One hundred and twenty degrees in the shade, enemies under every possible rock, and a constant state of anxiety. Dirty jokes and bullshit was how we got through it.

Then the whizz of a bullet flew parallel on the left side of the vehicle. And then all hell broke loose. Bullets fired from automatic weapons came from the left and the right—fucking canyons—and we had to scramble to respond. It was a quick firefight, maybe fifteen minutes, but Markhof took a bullet in the shoulder, just shy of his vest. It bled like a son of a bitch and Jones, rightfully, called for a medic. The fight was well over, most of the men lying dead or dying as their bodies tumbled down the hills.

The chopper landed, and Ria hopped out, looking beautiful and alive with a focused look on her face. Medic bag in one hand, she ran towards Markhof. "Forget to duck, Marky Mark?"

LOCKED

He grinned through the pain, his face a ghostly white. "Fucker was faster than me this time."

"Well, I'll stop the bleeding and then we'll make sure you a get a scar to impress the women who should know better."

Near unconscious, he gave her a thumbs up and closed his eyes. True to her word, Ria stanched the bleeding, and they got him into the chopper.

She gave me a wink and a smile, and said, "Stay safe, Texas Holden." She hopped back in and turned her focus back to Markhof as the chopper took off.

Twenty, maybe twenty-five seconds later, an RPG came from the hill to the right and hit its target. I watched as every piece fell to the ground. Every. Fucking. Piece.

They made us wait five hours to go in search of survivors, knowing there were none. Markhof, Ria, and the pilot, Randy, were nothing more than smoldering bits of carnage.

I hated that goddamn dream, and I hated even more that I didn't wake up until I was standing there over her dead body parts.

And the thing I hated the most was the hangover the next morning. At least I didn't have a long commute to Hardtail. I knew this land better than anyone. The first owner bought it about two weeks before I received my discharge papers from the Army, hired me on to tend his horses and cattle as soon as I came back.

The second owner gifted me some acreage at the south end of the property, and I built myself a little cabin. It wasn't much, a master bedroom and bath, a guest room and bath, a kitchen big enough to eat in, and a living room with a fireplace, but it was all mine. It was home.

And it was time for me to face the music, so I showered and dressed, choosing to delay coffee in favor of Martha's dark roast over at the big house. As soon as I stepped inside the kitchen, Peaches shoved a big mug in my hand.

"Morning!" she shouted with a wicked grin.

"Thanks for that." Yeah, if she was pissed, then Gunnar was pissed.

"Here you go, Holden." Martha handed me a plate piled high with biscuits, ham, and onions, and her special strawberry jam.

"Thanks, Martha. Nothin' better than your biscuits." She smiled and blushed before turning away, muttering something about charming cowboys.

"You were drunk last night." Gunnar didn't waste time with niceties, and the expression on his face could only be described as thunderous.

"I was, and I'm sorry."

"That's not good enough, Holden. Fuck! You know what kind of people our members are."

Yeah, I did. Rich and powerful people who liked to keep their kink on the down low. They paid big bucks for their privacy and a certain environment, which I understood. But . . .

"I know. It's no excuse, but I ran into someone from my past that I wish I hadn't, and it got to me. More than it should."

"Good," he said with a grim smile, "because you're working the bar again tonight just to prove to me you can."

Asshole. "That's bullshit, Gunnar."

"You wanted a plan. You got one."

Now I was pissed. "So this is what, revenge? That's bullshit, and you know it. Can you or any of the other guys handle the ranch duties without me? Who's gonna do all the chores that didn't get done this morning because I didn't get to bed until after three? Who's gonna do 'em tomorrow? Or did you hire an assistant like I asked you to six months ago?"

I didn't mind doing my part to help out at The Barn Door. Okay, I did mind, but I did that shit anyway because I gave my word *and* because it was lucrative as hell, but ranching was my thing. It was in my blood.

LOCKED

"If you weren't hungover you might have gotten up this morning." It was a weak argument, and even he knew it.

"With two goddamn hours of sleep? You try it and tell me how it goes. Anyone can work the fucking bar, and you know it. Not everyone can handle the cattle, never mind the horses. Especially Lady Mayhem."

Not even Gunnar had been able to tame the black Arabian who didn't like anyone but me.

"Then I guess you'll do your job tonight without the aid of Senor Patron."

Peaches snickered, and I glared at her, which only made her laugh harder.

"What the fuck ever." I stood and stacked what was left of the ham and onions into the last two biscuits, wrapped them in a napkin, refilled my coffee into a thermos and got the fuck on with my day.

KB WINTERS

Chapter Four

Aspen

"Don't be so uptight about it, babe." Ken stood in front of me wearing nothing but a pair of black and white polka dot briefs, a chub straining against the material as he thrust his hips in my direction. "Didn't you have fun last night?"

I rolled my eyes. "Do you think I had fun, Ken?"

Truthfully, my efforts at finding my own fun had fallen flat. Maybe I just wasn't as adventurous as I'd been in my twenties, or maybe I was just a bit more discerning. Whatever the reason, I ended up drinking more than I should have and watched the way people interacted with an interest I'd never had before.

He shrugged. "I don't know, Aspen, did you?"

"You did, and that's what matters, right?" I stood so his cock wasn't right in my face because there was no way in hell he was getting a blow job after asking me to go to a sex club again so he could fuck other women.

"It's not *all* that matters." He put a hand on my shoulder and rubbed it, a move that felt more like my old Uncle Milt than a lover.

"If you want, we can start the night off with a devil's threesome. You could take some dude's cock while I fuck you from behind. It could be real hot, babe."

Real hot, my ass. But was there really any point in arguing when I only had two choices. Trust him and let him go alone? Or tag along and make sure he didn't go too far over the line? What the fuck was *too far* over the line, anyway? Non-committal sex was better than him sneaking out and fucking around behind my back.

Wasn't it?

Was it?

Just then, a pair of killer blue-almost-black eyes flashed in my mind, that same hint of familiarity hovering in the back of my memories. I couldn't help but smile. Maybe that hunk was working tonight, and maybe he'd be my key to a little fun. If I could go through with it.

"Maybe I'll find my own fun, Ken."

His face lit up as my words registered. Any of the things a girlfriend should feel at the moment—disappointment, rage, hurt, self-consciousness—I didn't feel. All I felt was an odd sense of relief. And apprehension.

Ken felt none of those things. His face lit up, and he said, "Excellent! Shower quickie before we head out?"

A half-throb pulsed between my thighs. Enough to tell me I needed to get laid but not enough to work up the energy Ken's ego required lately. "You gonna make sure we both get off?"

"You know, Aspen, you're a fucking prude for someone who looks like a Barbie."

With an angry growl, he stomped into the bathroom and slammed the door behind him. A few seconds later, the shower sounded.

I shrugged to myself and thought, why am I with this asshole, anyway?

Ninety minutes later we entered the club, but tonight they featured a Heavenly Bodies theme, so said the doorman as he smacked the invisible stamp on the inside of my wrist. Unlike last night, they'd transformed the place into some kind of erotic celestial land, different shades of white in every imaginable fabric from silk to cotton to wool covering every surface and hanging from the ceiling. It was beautiful.

Sensual. And instead of the pulsing Latin beat, they had slow R&B music, the kind even kids in Texas played during first kisses, games of spin the bottle, and later, in the back of pickup trucks. Just below the music, I swear there was the sound of a man and woman moaning. Erotically.

"Gonna hit the head, babe. Be back soon." Ken smacked an absent kiss to my cheek and headed off, letting his hands and body graze against every woman he passed as he made his way downstairs. To the *rooms.*

But I wasn't in the mood to be in a bad mood. Not yet. So I shrugged off my annoyance, enjoyed the hot gyrating bodies, and even the not so hot ones, and made my way to the bar. Where, *sweet Lord yes,* the big man with the unforgettable blue eyes mixed the hell out of something in a silver cocktail shaker.

His biceps were big. No, they were huge, bending and flexing with every move. It was impossible to look away, and I didn't bother to hide my open ogling. This was a sex club, for crying out loud. People showed up in lingerie that hid nothing, so a little bit of ogling was fine.

After pushing my way through the crowd of groping hands, I finally made my way up to the bar, just a foot and a half of polished wood separated us. But he was either oblivious to my presence or ignoring me in favor of the drink order he handled quickly. And coldly. It gave me more time to examine him, to explore him.

My eyes roamed over his broad shoulders, strong arms, and wide chest. Gorgeous for sure, but not all that different from any other Texas cowboy. It was that smooth, sun-kissed skin and those almost haunting blue eyes that called out to me from my past. I jogged my memory for how I could know him, coming up with at least a dozen sets of eyes I'd rather forget permanently before I found it.

Found him, rather.

Holden Jennings. The only boy I'd ever had a serious crush on in high school. The one I never got to date. Not that I didn't get the opportunity, I did. It was just after high school graduation when he approached me. I was with my best friends Regina and Amber Leigh. Daddy was away on some big horse event, and Mama had gone with him even though it was my high school graduation. They'd left me a shiny red Mustang, though, so I guessed that was good enough.

Holden had grown into his shoulders since the last time I'd seen him. Back then he'd been all long arms and legs, and he wore a nervous smile as he approached in his dark jeans, cowboy boots, fancy shirt, and bolo tie. He'd opened his mouth, flashed that killer smile, and asked me out.

LOCKED

But I let peer pressure get to me, the sound of Amber Leigh snickering behind me, and Regina whispering that he was poor, which was a joke. His family wasn't poor. They just weren't as wealthy as mine. Turning him down was still one of my biggest regrets, and why I assumed the universe was punishing me with guys like Ken.

But now that I knew it was Holden, I had to say something. Didn't I? I mean, what were the odds that I'd run into my high school crush so far from Vance, and after all these years? When he was done handing over the final drink, I leaned forward with my most charming smile. "Holden Jennings, right?"

The dark look he gave me said maybe he remembered me too.

Shit.

KB WINTERS

Chapter Five

Holden

Lord give me the strength. That was as far as I got in making a deal with the universe before Aspen leaned over the bar and right into my line of sight.

"Holden Jennings, right?" As if she didn't know who I was, the flash of guilt in her smile told the truth.

Tonight she wore a dress that showed off a lot of skin but revealed nothing about her. A deep red color that matched her lips, long see-through sleeves, the dress barely hit mid-thigh, but the front and back of the dress held deep vees that made a man's fingers itch to touch, his mouth water to taste.

Not me, but most men. At least the ones who didn't know her.

"What can I get you to drink?" I gave her a bored look and waited before adding, "Absinthe cocktails are half off tonight."

"It is. Oh my God, Holden Jennings, it *is* you. It's me, Aspen Holt." Her pale blue eyes looked almost clear tonight, but they wore that same *queen of the universe* certainty they always held. She was so sure I'd remember her, but not just remember her, also that I'd be thrilled to see her again.

After how she treated me, I wasn't thrilled at all.

"About that drink? You're not the only customer in this joint, lady. Aspen," I corrected with enough acid in my voice to let her know, yeah I remembered her. As if I could ever forget that she was responsible for one of the most humiliating moments of my life. It was high school, ages ago, I know, and I should get over it. Hell, I *was* over it, but seeing her in my face pretending like none of it happened was enough to drive a man to drink. Only this man couldn't drink until he was off the clock.

Her confidence had slipped, but I estimated it was still at about eighty percent since she hadn't given up and gone down to Hazel's end of the bar.

"I'll have something with absinthe and bourbon."

LOCKED

Aspen had been a girl who knew her place in the world, and she was comfortable with everything it had afforded her, including beauty, wealth, and privilege. What was more, back then she'd been convinced she deserved it. I always wondered if she thought she deserved it because she was somehow *special*.

I didn't give much of a damn when it came to the woman in front of me. "Coming right up," I said and grabbed a glass I gave it an absinthe rinse the way Hazel showed me earlier and went about making the drink. I'd have to tell her later she was right about the absinthe. The stuff tasted vile to me, but everyone had been taking advantage of the deal.

"Do you remember me? Last night I wasn't sure how I knew you, but your eyes were familiar. I never forget a pair."

I snorted at what was clearly a line. She either had a selective memory, or she was hoping I forgot. "You don't have to bullshit me, sweetheart. It ain't required to make you a drink."

She sucked in a breath, offended or outraged, maybe a bit of both. "I'm just trying to have a conversation." She sounded so reasonable that to anyone listening, I'd come across like a real asshole.

Well, good, because I *was* a real asshole. "Is that right, Ms. Aspen Holt?"

"It is." She tilted her chin in the air defiantly, but I caught the tremble in her bottom lip and that flash of uncertainty in her eyes.

"Why would I want to talk to the woman when the girl I knew was such a bitch?"

She at least had the grace to flush with guilt. Or maybe anger at being called out. "Look, I'm sorry about that, but if—"

"This cocktail is right up your alley, Aspen. It's called The Billionaire." My words cut her off, and I slid the drink across the bar with more force than I meant to. "Enjoy."

I turned to walk away, but her words stopped me. "You won't even let me explain?"

LOCKED

I shouldn't have done it, but I did. I turned and looked at Aspen straight on. She was just as beautiful as I remembered, only now there was a bit of wisdom and cynicism that spoke of a life that hadn't gone as perfectly as she expected. It made her more beautiful if I was honest. Which is why I couldn't indulge myself like this with her.

"Nope. Your boyfriend seems to be looking for you. Better hurry. He seems like the type to get easily distracted."

I didn't bother telling her this wasn't the second time he'd come to the club because it wasn't my business.

"You're an asshole, you know that?"

I grinned. "No, I didn't. So I guess I'll have to take your word for it. Ma'am." I gave her an imaginary tip of my invisible hat, and with a groan, she snatched her glass and walked away. I stood there and enjoyed the view. Her legs looked spectacular in red fuck-me heels. They made her ass look like it was still high and round. It was too bad they belonged to her because those were exactly the kind of legs I enjoyed wrapped around my waist, my shoulders, or straight up in the air. Heels on.

"Enjoy your evenin'," I called after her, feeling satisfied when her steps faltered.

Chapter Six

Aspen

Holy shit. The drink Holden made was strong! It was good but so strong that my legs already felt a little wobbly as I stumbled my way through the crowd toward Ken, who was really looking for me. Even my clumsy steps didn't stop me from sucking back more of the cocktail, but I needed to get away from Holden. He'd been such a sweet boy back when I knew him.

Clearly, that guy was long gone.

It was too bad because I had such a huge crush on him in high school. And unlike all the other boys, he didn't fawn over me. No, Holden Jennings wasn't the fawning type. He was a typical, quiet cowboy, but he looked. A lot. And I always felt like he'd seen me, and I wanted him to see more. But when I had my chance, I blew it. I let my friends convince me that the high school pecking order mattered after we got our diplomas. What a stupid girl I was.

Was? My conscience would have laughed at that. Being with Ken, and here with him to boot, proved I was still that same stupid girl, doing the wrong thing for no good reason.

By the time I made it to the staircase that led to the playrooms downstairs, Ken had disappeared, and I couldn't find one ounce of disappointment about it. *Fuck Ken,* I decided. He could go and do what he would do, whether I wanted him to or not.

Why the hell shouldn't I do the same? Or at least maybe flirt a little with a few of the beautiful people in attendance tonight. Still, it didn't feel completely right, so I decided to find Ken first. Maybe this place would make things feel good again if we did it together.

Maybe we'd let someone watch.

Maybe.

I started with the rooms from the previous night, thinking he might have gone back there since he had some luck. Of course, Ken was never satisfied with the same *anything*. He liked to change it up and often, so I went to the opposite end of the hallway and started there.

First, I found the room dedicated to bondage. Though full, Ken wasn't among the men bent over, tied up, or whipping a willing partner. He wasn't even among the half a dozen or more men watching from the sidelines, cocks in their hands, stroking to the action.

Only one couple occupied the dungeon room, each of them focused intensely on nothing but one another and their pleasure. They seemed oblivious to the onlookers inside the room, hidden in the darkness, watching as he fastened metal clamps to her nipples. My nipples hardened in response.

When he fixed a clamp on her clit, the tiniest gasp of pleasure sounded in the room followed by several ecstatic groans. The couple made the most erotic picture; hell it was almost romantic, the way the man's eyes feasted on the woman. Every breath she took, every sound she made, he was perfectly aware of what she needed. What she wanted.

Fuck. I would've loved to give up control like that. My pussy throbbed, and I stood there and watched. Drenched.

Eventually, I moved on after realizing that the couple was serious about prolonging the pleasure. Like they were building up to something ethereal. Fifteen minutes later and no one but the onlookers were close to orgasm, so I moved on. To the orgy room.

Maybe I'd be adventurous for an ass-fucking.

It was a big room, at least double the size of all the other playrooms, enough that at least three orgies were happening at once. The left corner of the room looked like an expensive living room apartment paneled off to three sections. The largest section was a lavishly appointed bedroom, and the front area was dressed up as a backyard. No less than five people were in each room, as many as eight in the living room, all naked, with mouths and cocks and pussies and tits bare and exposed for the sole benefit of pleasure.

That was where I found Ken, in the huge circle of men who wanted to watch but weren't quite brave enough to join in, maybe in case they didn't match up to the bigger cocks on display. His cock was on display, though. His hand stroked it slowly, and even from my weird side angle, I could see his eyes lit with an excitement I hadn't seen in months. The worst part was, I couldn't tell if it was from watching the petite blonde take a huge black cock in her ass, or if it was that ripped ginger shoving his cock into the black guy's ass that had him so aroused. Even worse? I didn't give a damn. With Ken, it was always hard to tell because his sexual proclivities were hard to pin down.

His porn preferences didn't always match up with real life, but even his own comments were sometimes at odds with what he wanted and other than sticking to my personal limits, I didn't bother myself with that.

It said a lot about our relationship that I really didn't want to think about, so I took another gulp of my drink and watched Ken. I kept my gaze mostly focused on him to see what it was that made me stick around. He wasn't the wealthiest man I'd ever dated, nor the most attractive or charming. But I still spent the past year with him, even moving to Opey a few months ago.

Ken was secretive, but I was okay with that because he didn't ask a lot of questions about what I did all day. Not that I did anything beyond grooming and thinking, but the fact that he wasn't always asking questions made it easier to be around him. Especially lately.

It felt like we'd both given up but hadn't decided to end it yet, which was depressing. We were both young and attractive. It was far too early to settle, wasn't it?

A blonde woman from the bedroom area walked a straight line towards Ken, still slowly stroking his cock. I didn't blame her. Ken had a beautiful cock, seven inches, and just thick enough to feel good without making me sore the next day. He just wasn't overly focused on anyone's pleasure but his own. She stood in front of Ken, wearing nothing but a coy smile before she dropped to her knees.

LOCKED

Instead of being angry, I watched with a curious fascination as she wrapped one hand around his cock and slowly, tentatively licked the swollen head. Big eyes looked up at him as she licked him like a lollipop, drawing groans from more than just Ken. Finished teasing, she took him to the back of her throat once, twice, three times before his entire body vibrated.

"Fuck!" he moaned and wrapped her high ponytail around his fist, his brown gaze on hers as he plowed his cock down her throat while she smiled and took it, squeezing his ass as if to beg for more. This was a Ken I'd never seen before. He had a dark intensity as he held her, fucking her mouth but not callously so. No, he was almost gentle in the way he fucked her mouth and her throat, making sure she had that same gleam in her eyes that he did. Strangely, she did.

When Ken and I had sex, which was rare since we came to Opey, it was almost mechanical. I rarely gave him head since he refused to return the favor, and because he was such a selfish lover, I refused to share his kinks. There was no way I'd let him paddle my ass and *still* not have an orgasm. But this Ken was different. He actually gave a damn that the woman enjoyed having her throat fucked as much as he enjoyed fucking it. More than anything else I'd seen Ken do in The Barn Door, that was a hard pill to swallow.

They were intense together. Hot as fuck, honestly, and his hips moved faster and faster. She gripped his thighs and pushed him deeper down her throat before one hand moved to his balls and tugged.

"Oh, fuck!" he mouthed.

The blonde held his ass tight, keeping him close as he came down her throat, in sharp, violent shakes. She gave a dramatic swallow and stood, flashing a wink before she left the room.

Oddly, I didn't feel any anger at what I saw, just a vague sense of disappointment and arousal. I wanted what had just taken place between Ken and that random woman. I began to realize that maybe I wouldn't get it with Ken, the same way he clearly couldn't get it from me.

Chapter Seven

Holden

I didn't know what pissed me off more, that Aspen had the balls to approach me like we were old fucking friends, or that I was still thinking about her hours later. I shouldn't be thinking about her at all. She was nothing to me. Less than nothing. She was a customer, and I was forced labor. For one more night, anyway. If Gunnar made me do this shit again, I'd pack up and put Opey in my rearview mirror.

Fuck that. I wasn't going anywhere. I had a few acres and a home of my own, Opey was home. Which meant I had to suck it all up and be a fucking trooper for the rest of the night. Then tomorrow I'd get my ass up early and get back where I belonged. Ranching.

"Take a break, Holden." Hazel's voice broke through my thoughts, and I nodded, tossing the bar towel into a bucket that I picked up to take with me.

She laughed. "Doing your best to look like an employee?"

"Hell, yeah. Not that it's stopped 'em." These women were bold as hell, going after what they wanted in a way that would have had me rock hard, if I was into public sex. I wasn't. Or shittin' where I ate. Which I wasn't.

"Aw, boo-hoo. Horny ladies want to touch you."

I didn't even bother responding with words, just a glare to let her know she was annoying me. Break time meant I could relax my shoulders and put my feet up inside the employee break room. Away from the music and the people. Having so many people was good for business, which meant it was good for my cash flow, but goddamn, it was so many people. I preferred fewer people. Less noise.

Just less.

Everything.

It was the story of my life that shit never went the way it was supposed to, which is why I wasn't all that

LOCKED

surprised to set eyes on Aspen's boyfriend just ten feet away from my peace and quiet. Instead, I had to watch the little blond guy creep around in a way that could only be called suspicious, and that's what drew my attention. He was a newcomer to Opey. I kept my distance but watched closely as he tiptoed down the short hall that led to the romance room.

Even as I followed the guy, I figured I was just about to find another asshole cheating on his woman. And yeah, maybe it gave me the smallest thrill to know that woman was Aspen.

Inside the romance room, he greeted a leggy brunette with a kiss right on the mouth. It wasn't a simple greeting of old friends, though it was obvious this wasn't their first meeting. It was a tender greeting from the way he held her face to the way her fingers played lightly with the blond hair at the back of his neck. They were lovers as in present tense, as in perfectly in place inside the pink, red and white room filled with satin and lace and candlelight. A heart shape bed completed the look, with romance-themed sex toys lying all around.

I couldn't help the way my lips twitched thinking about the karma of it all. Yet, I couldn't even savor that thought because it only pissed me off more that I was thinking about Aspen. *Again.*

Aspen's man kissed his way down the brunette's body, slowly peeling the sexy lingerie from her tight little body, capped off with big, beautiful, fake tits. He licked and sucked the perky nipples that reached out for his touch as she arched into him, urging him to give her more. Which he did. He kept going, kissing down her flat stomach, only stopping to dip his tongue into her belly button, drawing a giggle from the woman. Then he was where they both wanted him, between her legs, lapping up her wet pussy like she was ice water on a scorching hot Texas day. Long, shapely legs wrapped around him as she ground against his face, his cock grew harder with every cry, every moan she made.

LOCKED

Maybe she just tasted that damn good. Maybe this was his woman, and Aspen was his mistress. Wouldn't that be something?

They were fucking now, hard and fast, intense as fuck with them eye-fucking each other as hard as their bodies slammed together. He didn't look away, not even once, as he pounded into her. Whatever was going on between them, he and the brunette were more than friends, more than lovers.

And none of it was any of my fucking business.

Now that I knew this guy had nothing to do with the trouble plaguing Opey, it was break time. Away from the freaks.

KB WINTERS

Chapter Eight

Aspen

"Yes! Oh, yes!"

It was the sound of pleasure, particularly of a woman's intense erotic pleasure that had my feet on the move, eager to see what kind of sex produced those sounds. A small crowd had gathered in front of the romance room, which was perfectly named. It was the exact room that every girl pictured as the backdrop to losing her virginity. It never was, of course. If she'd been lucky, it was a cheap hotel, and if not, the bed of some wannabe cowboy's daddy's truck. Somehow, all the pink and red hearts didn't look pervy or out of place at a sex club.

But the view inside the room was even more breathtaking than the room itself. A woman with long, wavy brown hair dropping down on a pink pillow while a man kissed his way down her back, drawing deeply erotic moans from her. At one point her head fell away to show off pink, kiss-swollen lips just as his lips reached the top of her ass. It was hot because it wasn't just fucking between them. That was obvious without even knowing anything about them. There was something real between these two; they were probably a couple who didn't mind others watching their love.

The man was nothing but a head of blond hair, his tongue slipping between the globes of her ass, licking down until he reached her pussy, sending her bucking away from him. "Yes, Ken, yes!"

Ken.

She said Ken. It was a common enough name, but the shiver of something that stole over me said it was Ken. My Ken. Hell, her Ken. Did that make him *our* Ken? Even as the thought came to me, his features came into focus, wispy blond curls that no amount of expensive hair product could tame. The small cluster of stars and diamonds tattooed between his shoulder blades sealed it. Her Ken was *my* Ken.

And my Ken was fucking another woman and this time, I was fucking pissed off.

LOCKED

Hell, I was more than pissed off. I was offended. Was I the kind of woman to let this shit happen to me, not just once, not twice, but three fucking times? No, I wasn't. Maybe I was still a small-town Texas girl at heart because I believed that I should leave with the one who brought me, as my granddaddy used to say.

"Ken," I banged on the glass. "You fucking piece of shit!"

This time, at least, his hips stopped pumping into her as his neck twisted in all directions to see where my voice was coming from. He found me when I stepped inside the room. And smiled. He fucking smiled. "Aspen, babe. Want to join us?"

"What the fuck do you think, Ken?" I felt like the biggest idiot in this place when he shrugged.

"No boundaries, babe. You knew what this place was and you know what I need." The challenge was there, in his eyes, and never in my life had I wanted to cause bodily harm to a person more than I wanted to at that moment.

So, I did. I picked up the closest thing to me, a big, rubber, purple double-sided dong, and I hurled it at the bed with all the strength and rage I could muster. "You asshole!"

It landed on his head and bounced off his shoulder before landing on the brunette's flat stomach and rolling off.

"Come over here right now. Take off your clothes and let Paige lick your pussy. You love that." He thought he could placate me, and that only made me want to throw something else.

So I did. This time it was a lamp. "Seems to me you don't have a problem eating pussy at all!"

He paled, and I knew in that moment we were so fucking over. We were the damn Civil War. Nothing, apparently not even cheating or dragging me to a damn sex club in the middle of the week could have hurt or angered me more. I wasted a year on this asshole with his dirty little kinks, his mediocre loving, and all because he lavished me with gifts and vacations. I ate it all up. Like a fucking fool.

LOCKED

"I'm so fucking stupid."

"Babe, chill."

"Chill? Fuck you! Ken." I found something else, a red-soled stiletto that looked exactly like the pair I had and hurled it at him with as much energy as I could.

"What the fuck, Aspen? Take your drunk ass home."

That piece of shit. I wasn't drunk enough to stop myself from lunging at Ken but someone or maybe it was something, hooked me around my waist and yanked me back in mid-air.

"What the hell? Put me down!" I tried to look over my shoulder at the guy behind me, but it was dark, and he was strong. Scary strong.

"I'm tossing your pretty little ass out of here and calling the cops."

"Holden?" The fight went out of me at the sound of his voice, And though I knew I shouldn't have been, I was glad to see him. Glad it was him and not some stranger who'd found me looking less than my best, behaving even worse than that.

"Calling the cops? For what?" I ignored the way my nipples grew harder every time his breath hit my neck.

"Assault. Attempted assault. Vandalism. Property destruction. Disturbing the peace. We don't tolerate this behavior in here, no matter who your daddy is." His tone was icy and dry. I guess it was some small comfort that he wasn't taking any pleasure in watching me fall so fucking low.

But it was the mention of my father, of his importance, and his reputation that took the last bit of energy from me.

"You can't call the cops. I'm not usually like this. Holden. You know me."

"I don't really care, sugar."

Sugar. It was such a Texas thing to say that it should have annoyed me, but coming from him, it sounded sweet. Almost endearing.

LOCKED

"I know you don't, but it's the truth."

I knew he didn't give a damn, but it mattered to me. I was drunk and humiliated and maybe even the smallest bit heartbroken, and I needed him to know I wasn't the train wreck I seemed to be.

Chapter Nine

Holden

"If you say so, Aspen." I wasn't sure whether to believe her or not, but since her little antics had interrupted my break, I didn't much give a damn. I heard the sex and the screaming from the break room, but when furniture started to shatter, it was time to intervene. Which meant my break was over.

"Have a seat." I dropped her onto the slender bench inside the storage closet. It was the closest place I could think of to get her away from her ex without dragging her out of the club and calling the law.

She plopped down on the bench with a pout as she struggled to find a comfortable way to sit that didn't show off everything. I was happy to watch her squirm for once. "You don't believe me."

"Does it matter what I believe?"

The last bit of air deflated out of her at my words. I felt a twinge of sympathy for her.

"I guess it shouldn't, but for some reason it does." Her shoulders hunched forward in defeat, and all the anger seemed to have fled her pale blue eyes.

"I guess I wanted you to think I'd grown up. Matured."

She was looking for sympathy, and unfortunately for me, I was close to feeling it for her.

"Legally allowed to drink and make bad decisions. That's officially an adult, isn't it?"

She flashed a half-smile that spoke of a woman who could now laugh at herself. At least a little, and it was endearing, dammit.

"True enough," she said, but the words came out barely above a whisper. "I guess, hell I just don't know, Holden."

Her last words came out on a sob, just one at first. Then another and another until her delicate shoulders trembled under the force of her tears. "I'm sorry about…this."

LOCKED

Ah, shit. Just because she rejected me a million years ago in high school didn't mean I had to return the favor when she was obviously hurting and going through some shit.

"Ah, hell Aspen, don't cry. He ain't worth it."

No one was worth the kind of tears she was shedding for that dickwad.

"I know that," she screamed, but it didn't have any energy or fire behind it.

"That's why I'm crying." Her shoulders shook and kept on shaking, and I felt hopeless as hell. "What am I even doing with him?"

Good question, but I figured she didn't really want the answer because it was clear as day. The guy was clearly rich and probably made up for love and affection with expensive gifts.

"Ken's exactly who you thought you'd end up with, right?" At least, from all appearances, that was what everyone thought. He looked like all the guys she'd dated in high school. Handsome in that catalog kind of way; well dressed like he bought his outfits right off the mannequin. They were all rich, privileged assholes who majored in bullying the less fortunate.

Aspen huffed out a laugh. "I guess guys like Ken are my punishment from God." Her words were starting to slur.

I was too surprised at her admission to say anything but the obvious. "Yeah? Punishment for what?"

"For saying no to you when I wanted to say yes. For not being strong enough to withstand the peer pressure of my so-called friends. For not being brave enough to do something about crushing on the wrong guy."

Shit. Why did she have to go and say that?

"Ah, Aspen." I didn't know whether to be offended, relieved, or flattered.

"I'm sorry, Holden. For everything." What a pathetic sight she made. Instead of being happy or even a little fucking joyful, I felt bad for her. Poor little rich girl and I was fucking buying it. She started to slump over, and I reached forward to grab her.

"It ain't all bad, Aspen. You'll leave him and find another rich prick real soon, and maybe he'll buy you bigger jewelry and better vacations."

I was being an asshole, and I knew it, but I needed to protect myself ,dammit.

She laughed as she stood and the sound was loud, and rich, feminine. "You might be right, but that's the funny part. Ken didn't give me anything I couldn't have gotten for myself. How pathetic am I?"

She wasn't pathetic at all, but now that all of her weight was pressed up against me, starting with big fleshy tits, I couldn't think of a damn thing to say. Not that it mattered since she was pretty much passed out on her feet. If I moved, even an inch, she'd fall over and hit her pretty little head.

"You'll be all right, Aspen."

A yawn escaped when she looked up and flung an arm over my shoulder or tried to but the height difference made that impossible.

"It's good to see you again, Holden. I missed your smile." Seconds later, a soft snore sounded and I groaned. Stuck in a storage closet with my drunk high school crush who was nursing a broken heart.

The universe had a cruel, twisted sense of humor.

Chapter Ten

Aspen

Waking up to the sound of little men in suspenders pounding drums inside my head was not what I had in mind when I went out last night. The fuzzy mouth and swollen tongue told me I was dehydrated, but whatever light was shining on the other side of my eyelids, was too much for me to open up and search for water. I was still dressed in my clothes from the club, which meant I drank too much to undress, and I probably went to sleep with my makeup on.

All signs pointed to a hangover, which brought back some of the memories from last night. Ken fucking that brunette. Paige he said her name was, so tenderly. Bitch. Fucking her in a way he never, not once, not even on our six month anniversary, fucked me. And, oh yeah, he ate her pussy. Ate her fucking pussy when I couldn't even get one tiny little lick.

I sighed. "Asshole." I was ready to fuck him up.

But, I didn't feel like I was on my own bed, and it was too quiet. No matter how much it stung, I forced my eyes open and looked at my surroundings. I was in a cabin, with high ceilings and oversized logs that made up the walls.

A fucking log cabin.

A weird feeling crept into my belly. *Where am I? Chained to the bed?* That possibility stopped me in my tracks.

I sat up. And let out a breath. I was being ridiculous. Thankfully, this cabin didn't belong to a serial killer. No chains, just a nice, spacious king size bed. It probably belonged to one of Ken's shady sex friends, so I slid off the bed, grabbed my shoes and purse, and opened the door.

The place was so damn quiet. The only thing I could hear was the sound of my heart slamming against my chest. I held my breath and turned left, hoping that

LOCKED

was the way out, though what the hell I'd do when I got there was anyone's guess.

Living room. And the front door was only a few feet away, but a form on the sofa stole my focus. Dammit. Holden. Of course, this was his place with its big cedar logs, high ceilings, and equally high windows that let in plenty of light. Simple, homey but sturdy furniture covered in some kind of checkered flannel said this was a lived-in home, not the showpieces Ken's friend's preferred. This place was by contrast, understated.

More incredible than the sense of home this place created was the man on the sofa. Holden Jennings. Damn, he was a sight to behold, and with his shirt off, he was breathtaking. He had muscles everywhere. Some of his muscles even had muscles. Gone was the gangly boy I remembered, replaced by a man with broad chest muscles tipped with pink nipples.

Pale skin couldn't hide eight rippling ab muscles or the deep vee that faded into jeans that rode too low to keep my thoughts from going places they shouldn't.

A light coating of black hair dusted across his chest before turning into a thicker, darker trail that disappeared behind his button. And Lord knows what else. I didn't have to imagine what was behind that zipper because I'd heard the rumors in high school.

I couldn't help but think that was what a man should look like. My mouth watered, and even my pussy woke up, despite how early in the morning it was and how gross I felt.

"This ain't on the menu, sweetheart."

That deep sexy drawl startled the hell out of me. I blinked, letting my gaze take its time crawling up his body before settling on those blue eyes, dark and sleepy.

"I was just debating whether or not to wake you since you look so peaceful. And because you're nice when you're out cold." Nice to look at, anyway.

He laughed, and the sound came out kind of rusty, like he wasn't used to laughing much and that thought made me sad. Holden, the boy I knew, was meant to spend his life laughing. I wondered what had happened to steal his joy, but I wasn't stupid enough to ask.

"Since I'm already up, decision made. What do you need first, shower, food, or home?"

Instead of answering his question, I frowned. "How did I get here?"

Holden sat up. Abs flexed, I had to fight back a moan, which he, thankfully, didn't notice. "I couldn't find your date after you fell asleep."

"I passed out?"

"In my arms inside the supply closet at the club," he said matter of factly. I appreciated the lack of judgment. "Security said they saw him leave while we were in there, and you were too out of it to offer up any useful information."

"What information did I offer up that wasn't useful?"

I was afraid of the answer, but I needed to know. If I humiliated myself, then I deserved it. Thirty-three was too old to drink like that.

He shrugged. "You said you missed my smile."

That wasn't so bad. "I didn't realize how much until I saw it. You were always laughing and smiling back then." He hadn't been rich like most of my friends, but he seemed happier. "Thank you for looking after me, Holden."

"I just put you in my bed and set a bucket beside you. Hopefully, there's no puke in my bed?"

His bed? "Why did you give me your bed?"

"The other one has no bedding, and I can sleep anywhere, thanks to the Army."

He shrugged again as he stood like it was no big deal when what he'd done was a big damn deal. Men didn't just help out vulnerable women without taking a little bit for themselves, at least not the men I knew.

"There was no puke, not that I saw, but the bed is so damn big it could be anywhere." Holden's arms went high in the air as he stretched, drawing his muscles tight so that I could see him in all his glory. Pale, rippling muscles highlighted by ebony hair. My tongue slid across my lips.

"Eyes up here, Aspen." I heard the amusement in his voice despite his hard tone.

Right. Shit. "Uhm, I think I'll take that shower you offered first, please." I turned and darted back down the hall, the deep gravelly sound of Holden's laughter following me.

To keep myself from thinking about Holden, which would likely lead to me touching myself... in his shower, while thinking of him, I rushed through the shower. I didn't think about the fact that using his body wash meant I'd smell like him, sexy and earthy and masculine as hell. I didn't think of how my hair would smell like his. I washed, and I rinsed, and I got the hell out, wrapped in a towel and wishing I hadn't drunk so much last night.

It was one thing to do the walk of shame after a long night filled with orgasms. It was another after a dissatisfying trip to a sex club. In ultra slutty clothes. Scooping my clothes up off the floor, I took them out of the steamy bathroom and into Holden's bedroom. And stopped short.

"What are you doing?" Cashing in on his good deed, no doubt.

One brow quirked just the tiniest bit, and I knew he didn't miss the way I gripped my towel even tighter. "Those are for you. From Peaches."

No wonder he didn't make a move. "Wife or girlfriend?" I didn't want to think about that pang of disappointment in my belly, so I called it hunger. Hangovers always made me hungry.

"Gunnar's wife to be. She said they'd be too big, but I figured you'd rather have something fresh to wear."

Less trashy was probably what he meant but was too nice to say because, despite his rudeness, Holden was a good southern boy.

"Thanks." I practically ran over to the bed to inspect what Peaches had sent over. It was simple and guaranteed to fit, a simple pink tank dress, and she even included a belt to cinch the waist. And underwear, though I wasn't sure how I felt about wearing another woman's panties, never mind a stranger's. Since beggars couldn't be choosers, I decided to go commando.

Feeling Holden's gaze on me, I glanced over my shoulder, and sure enough, he was still standing there leaning against the door frame, taking up nearly every available inch. Staring at me.

A shiver tore through me at the heat in his eyes. "Yes?"

His grin came slowly, and it was dark. Intense. "I was waiting for my show," he said gruffly, but even that didn't mask the heat in his eyes.

It was a challenge. I knew that. And, damn him, it was one I couldn't resist. It helped that Holden didn't think I would, so I stood just a little bit taller and looked him right in those deep blue eyes, feigning innocence.

"A show?"

Was he messing with me or did he expect a payment for services rendered?

"Yeah, just like the one you got earlier."

For some odd reason, his request had me feeling nothing but relief. He didn't expect anything in return for his help last night, just the way I ogled him earlier.

"Right." There was something almost endearing about his bad attitude, the honesty of it if not the attitude itself. "A show."

I was ready to do this, and with one little flick of my thumb, the towel fell away, giving him a good long glimpse of me in all my glory. I looked damn good, and I knew it.

"You look great for a chick over thirty," as Ken always said.

God, he was such an asshole.

But Holden looked at me like I was scorching hot. Like he was staring at my high school body with perky tits and a flat stomach, not ten, okay twelve extra pounds. He sucked in a breath, and his nostrils flared as his gaze scanned over my body. Once.

Twice.

Three times.

Then his eyes took a fourth sweep, and I nearly moaned out loud.

He didn't want to, but he couldn't look away. That heat mixed with anger was a powerful, palpable thing between us, hot and dangerous and dark. But mostly hot. Finally, he had enough and pushed off the wall.

"I'll be downstairs."

His bad mood made me grin. It was nice to know someone wanted me. Even if that someone hated me.

Chapter Eleven

Holden

Goddamn it. Why did I issue that stupid fucking challenge? I should have known that tangling with the prom queen wouldn't go my way this time any more than it had in the past. She'd seen through me and raised the stakes, giving me a long, long look at her spectacular body.

And it was fucking spectacular. Her tits were perfect teardrops, her nipples big and pink and hard. My mouth watered even now just thinking about it. It didn't help that we were crammed together inside my truck. It never escaped my attention that her gorgeous hot body grazed mine on the turns.

Aspen crossed her legs, and I thought about the treasure buried between those thighs, that strip of hair covering her pussy, and that glimpse of her slit I couldn't forget. Even though I preferred a bit more of a bush, I couldn't deny the need flaring through my cock to be buried between those bare pussy lips for a few hours.

Hell, maybe a few days.

Aspen sighed and turned to me, staring for a long time as she tried to figure me out. She'd been doing that since she found me drinking coffee in the kitchen and looking out at the land that was mine. All mine.

"Why are you helping me?"

That was what she wanted to know? I shrugged.

"Why not? You needed help, and I was in the position to give it."

Hell, even I didn't know why I was helping her, and I didn't plan on giving it much thought. Didn't have to. All I had to do was drop her off and then be on my way. Never to lay eyes on Aspen Holt ever again.

She sighed again, unhappy with my answer. "I really did have a crush on you back then, you know? Started sometime during junior year. You hit a growth spurt over the summer. You were over six feet with wide shoulders and a man's jaw. Your voice was really deep, and I was sure you'd ask me out since everyone else had. But you didn't." There was no accusation in her voice, just shock.

"Until I did." The words had more bite than I meant, and there was no point kicking a pup when it was already down. Even if it was a wolf pup. "I wanted to ask you out, but I saw the guys you dated and didn't think I stood a chance. I should have kept thinking that."

"I was stupid." She said it so plainly like it was just an accepted truth that it pissed me off. "You think Ken is my karma?"

Kind of. "No. I think Ken is an asshole. You don't treat a woman that way."

"Not even me?"

I sighed and risked a glance at her. "Have I ever treated you anywhere close to how he does?"

"No," she admitted, and her shoulders fell. "You were rude at first, but I deserved it, but now, you have been far nicer than I deserve."

I wasn't sure that was true. Her teenage self had been a bitch and crushed my heart, but a lot has changed since then. For both of us.

"You should try it sometime," is what I said instead. Dammit. "Sorry."

"No, you're probably right. Maybe I am just a terrible person, and that's why I end up surrounded by terrible people."

"Sounds like you got a lot of thinking to do. Good thing we're here." My voice was gruff because, dammit, she was starting to get to me, and I wouldn't be stupid enough to let her get to me again. Her or anyone else.

"You're right. Thanks for the ride. And for taking care of me. It was good to see you again, Holden." She sighed wistfully like she really meant it, and I felt like an asshole for wishing she'd hurry up so I could stop the invasion of her scent mingling with my shower gel and shampoo.

"Take care of yourself, Aspen." I hoped that she would because having seen her now, the beautiful mess that she was, I sincerely hoped she figured out what made her happy and went for it. She was too rich, too beautiful for that level of unhappiness.

"Thanks."

That one word held a depth of emotion, and I didn't want to think about it. Couldn't. Instead, I watched her walk up to the condo she shared with Ken. When I knew she was safely inside, I made my way back home.

To Hardtail Ranch.

Before I even put the truck in park, Gunnar was at my side.

"So, what did y'all find out last night? Anything?"

He yanked the door open and jumped in. "You should have seen what those assholes did to the Monroes. They may be horny old twins, but they didn't deserve the vandalism those motherfuckers laid down on their B&B. Wasn't a stick of furniture left standing."

Shit. Mary and Elizabeth Monroe were town treasures. And damn-near molesters, but they didn't mean anything by it. Now, they needed our help.

"Good thing we didn't catch the bastards last night," Gunnar said with a nasty growl. "They'd never walk again, and that would be for starters."

I put the truck in gear and said, "That's good enough for me. Let's go check things out."

I could tell I surprised him by the deer in headlights expression he wore before he blinked it away and gave a short nod.

"Lead the way," he said as he snapped on his seatbelt.

I revved the engine and left Hardtail for the second time that day.

It must be some kind of record because I preferred to stay close to home.

***

LOCKED

"I still can't get used to this shit." Gunnar wore a tight smile and waved at Big Mac in his denim overalls. "Everyone knows everyone."

I had to laugh. Gunnar had been in Opey long enough to get used to the friendliness of the townsfolk, but he was such a damn curmudgeon that it still surprised him. "More importantly, they know everything."

More than a few people had made some thinly-veiled comments about what we'd done to help the town, but I thought it was best to keep that from Gunnar.

After a quick circuit of the town, we pulled up to the giant blue and yellow Victorian that was the Opey Saloon & Lodging. Really, it was nothing more than an average small-town bed and breakfast. The sisters held court on one end of the wraparound porch.

"We were coming back from our late morning walk and found the place vandalized! Looks like a New

York City subway car," Mary said with great enthusiasm. "Remember our trip to the big apple, Liz?"

Liz, or Elizabeth as she was known to everyone else, nodded absently at Mary's words, gesturing for me and Gunnar to go inside before she joined us.

"Mary seems to be doin' all right," Gunnar noted to Liz as we stepped inside.

"Nah. She's got a lot of theatrics going on, but those trembling hands are more than age. It's fear."

"He's not wrong," Elizabeth said as she joined us. She slipped between us and headed straight for the kitchen, leaving us to follow.

"I sure am sorry this happened to you both," I said.

Elizabeth turned back to me with a grin. "You're a good boy, Mr. Holden. You too, Gunnar."

Gunnar tried to hold his surprise, but his eyes went wide when the old woman gave one of his biceps a good, obvious squeeze.

LOCKED

"Uh, thanks. Any idea who might have done this? Any recent guests who stick out?"

Elizabeth shrugged, her flirtatious demeanor subdued as she talked about the vandalism, busying her hands by putting on a pot of coffee. "Not particularly, no. A few rough types came through over the past few weeks, but this is cattle country and sometimes even cowboys need a bed, you know?"

I nodded because I did know. Sometimes a man craved the comforts of home, even if they were manufactured.

"Any of them stay long?" These guys had been in town long enough that they wouldn't be staying here.

"No, but, well, it's nothing really." Her hands shook, and I took the tray loaded up with the coffee pot, mugs, cream and sugar from her hands and set it on the table.

"Maybe it's nothing, or maybe it'll help. We won't know until you tell us."

She nodded and distracted herself with being a good hostess, pouring first Gunnar and then me, a full mug of coffee to go along with the coffee cake she produced out of nowhere.

She was nervous, shaken as she cut and served the cake.

"Is there cinnamon in this coffee?" Gunnar looked like a kid who'd found marshmallows in his hot chocolate.

Elizabeth gifted him with a proud smile as she sat. "And bourbon. It's my special recipe."

"It's perfect."

That seemed to relax her shoulders because she sat back in her chair and folded her hands on top of the table. "Thanks. There was this one guy, though, who stuck out. Everything about him screamed 'big city' no matter how much he tried to blend in here. Expensive jeans that probably never saw a speck of dust, brand new boots he didn't have the decency to scuff."

LOCKED

She thought for a long moment before she spoke again, Gunnar and me both leaned forward in anticipation of what she'd say next.

"This guy was more the type to cut my damn throat than ruin my possessions, know what I'm saying?" We shared a worried look. A guy who looked like that on the surface was probably a hitman. A pro.

The question wasn't just why, but who?

"Anyway, the weird part was that he checked out on Thursday and Friday morning I saw him meeting with that blond-headed businessman, some kind of developer he said he was. Internet or real estate, I don't know. But the guy who stayed here didn't seem to be in development, if you know what I'm saying."

Yeah, we both knew what Elizabeth was saying. Some shady shit was definitely going on in Opey, and it was more than the petty burglaries. Just like Gunnar thought. It was a lot to unpack, and the B&B wasn't the place, so I shoveled in two forkfuls of cake and groaned.

"Best coffee cake I've had since my grandmama passed, Elizabeth. I swear."

Her cheeks turned pink even as she leaned forward and let her index finger graze the top of my hand. "You flatter me," she said and waggled her eyebrows. The old lady made me blush.

"Oh Elizabeth, there you are!" Mary entered the kitchen, the same bundle of energy she always was. The woman woke up, turned her dial to ten, and didn't stop until her head hit the pillow at night. I was convinced of that.

"Oh, and with such handsome visitors." Mary winked at both of us, her green eyes lit with mischief.

"These nice boys were just asking some questions."

Mary leaned in, showing off seventy-year-old cleavage that, honestly, didn't look a day over fifty.

"I knew you boys would come see about things. I just knew you would." She patted my cheek, gratitude now darkening her gaze. "Thank you."

LOCKED

Gunnar looked uncomfortable and shocked at her words, or maybe it was the way her hand slid down his arm to cup his ass. "Uh, we haven't done anything, Mary."

"Not yet, you haven't, but I have faith that you will. Now let me cut you big, strong men another piece of coffee cake, this time the brown sugar rum, and I'll tell you some things you ought to know." Mary spoke with the authority she'd earned as one of the biggest gossips in Opey. That was saying a lot for a town that trafficked in gossip. Especially by women of a certain age.

We listened to all the details the twins dished out about every person who'd come in and out of town. Every person who struck them as odd or untrustworthy somehow. The old girls may have been born and raised in Opey but they knew people, and they had excellent instincts.

Three pieces of coffee cake later, Gunnar and I were finally free, and we did one final drive through before heading back to the ranch.

Tonight, nothing appeared to be out of the ordinary.

Chapter Twelve

Aspen

Curled up on the sofa with my tablet searching for apartments wasn't how I imagined I'd be spending the day, but I also hadn't expected Ken to stay gone for more than a week. Not that I was stewing or even pining for him, I wasn't. But his noticeable absence had finally highlighted my need to get my own place. It wasn't like money was a factor. It was, as Daddy had accused, laziness. Plain and simple.

But today, I was shrugging off the lazy nametag and getting down to business. Looking for apartments. Why I was looking in Opey, I had not one damn clue except for the fact that it was as good as any place with the added benefit that I was already here. Besides, if I got a short-term rental, I could leave in a hurry if things got too dicey in Opey.

Being at Holden's had kicked up thoughts and memories of home. Vance, Texas. It was as small town as small towns come, complete with just one stoplight, an old school diner, and a town crazy about football and rodeo. It was a great place for me to grow up. As the daughter of the richest and most influential man in town, it had its perks like the shiny new car I'd gotten on my sixteenth birthday and never ever seeing a lick of trouble, no matter how bad things got.

But it also came with disadvantages, namely living up to the Holt name. Too many responsibilities, too many obligations, and too many damn eyes watching everything I did.

Every-fucking-thing.

But there was something about Holden's place that made me forget all the eyes and remember only the great outdoors. Even the inside of his home, covered in cedar, summoned the most beautiful parts of Texas where the trees grew tall, and the sky went on forever. Outside though, there was a peace about the place that set my soul at ease. With a slight scent of horses and hay and grass in the air, for just a moment, it felt like the western end of Wrangled Heart Ranch where I grew

LOCKED

up. Not to mention that many of my memories of home were tangled up with Holden.

Holden Jennings. He'd grown up to be even yummier than when he was a boy. Even thoughts of the man he was today was enough to have me reaching for my vibrator, which I could do freely with Ken gone. Not that I had the desire, not with this feeling of unease that settled in my gut, a mixture of acid and sawdust that made simple things like eating and drinking difficult.

A knock on the door yanked me out of my head and into the present. The condo I shared with Ken was sterile and sophisticated, decorated in shade of beige and cream. A perfectly nice but blah condo. Walking the length of the living room, I opened the door and found a man dressed in all black, which on its own, wasn't all that remarkable. But the long sleeves, the combat boots, and the baseball cap marked him as an out of towner, but definitely not a tourist.

Everything about his outfit was the definition of nondescript, brown hair, brown eyes, average height and weight. Suddenly my instincts kicked in, and I gripped the doorknob.

But it was too late. He pushed inside, non-threatening, but still.

"Is there something I can help you with?"

I didn't bother hiding my annoyance since this guy had invaded my space, not the other way around.

The non-descript man stared at me, gave me a quick once-over before tossing a dismissive wave in my direction. "Ken. Where is he?"

Nice to meet you too, fuck face. "Your guess is as good as mine. Last I saw Ken he was balls deep in some brunette called Paige."

More information than this guy probably wanted, but again, my space and my time.

"When did you see him last?" The man was angry and quiet, but he had a lethal quality about him that gave me pause. "When?" he barked louder than he needed to, making me jump.

"Almost a week ago, jeez! No need to be an asshole about it." But this guy wasn't moved. He was an asshole, and it didn't bother him one bit. "Why are you asking all these questions?"

It should have been the first question out of my mouth but this guy wasn't the first to come around looking for Ken. Sometimes he forgot who he owed money to until they tracked him down.

"Your boyfriend," he began, but I cut him off.

Quickly. "Ex-boyfriend." He glared at me, and I shrugged. "It's true. What has he done now?" Because it was always something with Ken. Never anything big, just a serious of nuisances guaranteed to drive the average woman out of her ever-loving mind.

"Don't you worry about why I need to see him. When you see him let him know Farnsworth is looking for him."

I searched my mind for that name, and I came up blank. That didn't mean much, Ken had too many business associates to keep track of, and he preferred to meet with them in nightclubs, bars, and casinos. Not exactly my favorite hangout spots these days. Though I didn't recognize his face or his name, the man was inside an empty house. With me. My heart raced so fast I thought it might make it out of the condo before I did. I nodded slowly.

"I'll leave a note." The plan had been to find a place and move before Ken came back to avoid the drama. Now I saw it might have to be even sooner.

"Give. Him. The. Message." His voice was low and menacing, his look dark and threatening. Angry.

"I won't be here, Farnsworth. Ken is your problem now, not mine."

I wasn't his goddamn secretary. If he didn't get the message, that wasn't on me.

But Farnsworth wasn't convinced. His brown eyes turned black, and I swear his face turned red with rage as he stormed towards me, getting in my face to intimidate me. His chest pressed against mine until my shoulder blades dug into the wall, and he pulled out a six-inch blade from behind him and pressed the tip to the hollow of my throat.

I tried to ignore my pulse fluttering against the blade, unaware of how dangerous such a natural act was at the moment.

"Maybe you misunderstood me." He applied the slightest pressure to my neck with a sick smile. "Tell Ken that Farnsworth is looking for him. If he doesn't get the message, I'm holding you responsible."

I scoffed, but the knife pressed harder to my throat, and a yelp escaped when the skin broke. One drop of blood trickled down my chest and soaked into the neckline of my tank top.

"Whatever image your pretty head is conjuring up about what you think I'll do to you, I'll do a thousand times worse." His hips pressed into mine, making sure I felt the swell of his cock pressed right between my legs. "Understand?"

How could I not? A quick nod with my eyes closed, and finally, I could breathe again. "Got it."

"Good." He slid the knife back into a sheath that disappeared into the back of his boot. "If I have to come back, I'll bend you over the couch and fuck you in the ass while Ken watches."

I snorted at the imagery. "Ken would probably get a kick out of that. Maybe you should do it to Paige. He seems actually to give a shit about her."

The man, Farnsworth, was not amused. He turned a look on me, so dark and menacing it made me shiver. "Then I guess I'll have to find more creative incentives." The gleam in his dark eyes terrified me. The moment he left; my feet moved into action.

Into the bedroom to pack two bags as quickly as I could and with as many of my belongings would fit in one trip. I did what I should have done the day Holden dropped me off here. I left.

For good.

***

LOCKED

I had a problem with never staying in any one place for too long; I didn't have anyone to call on when I really needed an ear. Or a hug. Or refuge. Sure, I could do another turn around the block and hop on the freeway headed to Vance with my tail between my legs, apologizing and letting Daddy strut about like a peacock for being right.

I can just hear him now. "Monty is still single, you know."

The thought of that conversation made me throw up a little, and I shook off all thoughts of Vance, of my mama, and my younger twin sisters. Vance was a last choice, one I couldn't in good conscience use. It could put my family in danger, so I drove around Opey.

Aimlessly.

Some thugs had recently vandalized the B&B, so I had to find a hotel for the night. But first, I had a stop to make. Hardtail Ranch. But I went in through the front gate because this visit had nothing to do with Holden. Nothing at all.

I threw my Beemer into park and stepped from the car with the clothes wrapped in paper. Another little quirk of a small town dry cleaners, adorable personal touches like hand-wrapped paper around freshly pressed clothes. The sun was shining bright so all I saw were the curves and the wild curls of the person on the porch.

"I hope you're the woman I came to see."

She quirked a brow, and I realized she probably had no idea who the hell I was. "Oh yeah?"

"Yeah. Peaches, right? Sorry, I'm Aspen, and you let me borrow some clothes last week that I wanted to return." I held up the package, like an idiot.

"I'm Peaches," she said simply. "You didn't have to get them dry cleaned."

"It was the least I could do."

She looked at me. Stared hard but not with the hardness of one woman judging another. Just a basic assessment to see if I was a threat to her or anyone in her orbit. It was a look as foreign to me as the moon, but like good art, I knew it when I saw it.

"I appreciate it, either way. Come on inside," she said and went in without waiting for me to answer. It was an impressive move, take charge without being bossy.

"I can't stay. I have to get going." Where the hell I was going, I hadn't a clue, but after that visit by the man in black I wasn't sure staying in Opey was a smart move.

"Where are you going?"

"Out of town. For a while." It wasn't a lie. Probably.

"Family?"

"No," I sighed. "Things are a little strained with my family these days, and it's all my fault." It was a hard pill to swallow, that Daddy had been right. *Again.* "No. I just need to…go."

Again, she gave me one of those long, studying looks as if she could see right down to my soul, and then nodded. "Coffee?"

"Uhm, sure. Thanks."

"Just finished brewing," she said, setting the pot on a decorative stone on the table along with sugar and cream. "No offense but you don't seem like The Barn Door type."

I didn't know if that was a compliment or not, and I was too tired to figure it out, so I went with honesty.

"I'm not. I went because I didn't want Ken, that was my boyfriend, to fuck other girls. Turns out my presence wasn't much of an obstacle."

Why I thought it was, again, I had no idea.

"Shit, that's rough. I'm sorry."

"Don't be. You know how, when you want to clean the house and you have to move shit from one place to the other? And then when you get there, you have to move shit there as well so you just say fuck it and live in a messy house?"

LOCKED

I didn't wait for her to answer.

"That's how my relationship with Ken was. If it wasn't one thing, it was another. All clues that we weren't right for each other until they were impossible to ignore."

It felt good to get that out, even if it was in front of a complete stranger.

"Sorry. Thanks for the coffee."

"Why are you leaving so fast?"

I wasn't sure if I could trust her, then again, I didn't trust anyone—not anymore. But the word around Opey was that the guys at Hardtail Ranch were military veterans and some kind of gang who kept the town safe. Protected.

"One of Ken's friends showed up looking for him, and he wasn't exactly nice about it." Even thinking about the way he touched me, the way his cock was hard and pressing against me, made me slam my eyes shut and shiver. It wasn't an actual assault, I didn't think, but I wasn't over it. Not yet.

"Whoa, what's wrong?" I opened my eyes and found Peaches much closer with concern swimming in her beautiful eyes. "What did he to do to make you cry?"

Cry? I wiped under my eyes, and sure enough, there were tears. "It was nothing. He j-j-just scared me a little, that's all. It's nothing."

"If it's nothing, why are your hands shaking and why are you still crying?"

I shook my head and stood. "I'm not. It's just been a long couple of weeks." More like a long couple of years. "Really, I just wanted to drop the clothes off. Thanks for your hospitality."

"For crying out loud woman, take a damn seat." Peaches shook her head, wild curls bouncing around her face even as she brought the coffee mug to her lips. "What did this friend of Ken's do to you? Exactly?"

"Nothing," I assured her, shaking my head and feeling silly. "I don't know why it shook me up. Really."

LOCKED

I gave her a quick rundown of what happened, a shaky smile on my face. "No big deal."

"It's a big damn deal, Aspen. A really big deal."

"No." It really wasn't. "It doesn't matter because I don't ever plan on seeing him or anyone else named Farnsworth ever again. Ever. That guy gave me the creeps with a capital C."

"Farnsworth?" Her voice changed when she said the name, and my gaze found hers. "That's what he said his name was?"

"Yeah. You know him?"

"Not now, but I once knew someone with that name. Wasn't a good guy either."

"Another name added to the list of men to avoid." Maybe tucking my tail between my legs wouldn't be so bad. At least Daddy would be able to keep me safe. But there's no way in hell to contain the twins. They were me in high school with better clothes, better technology, and double the bitch.

"Too bad you're a city girl. I could get Gunnar to hire you around here if I could justify it."

"Despite appearances, I am not a city girl. Born and raised in Vance, not far from Holden, in fact." Her eyes flashed, and I knew I'd given her a new piece of information. "But I don't need a job, and I've done my time mucking stalls."

She shrugged. "From what I understand, everyone mucks stalls."

"They do. I did, from the time I was big enough to hold a shovel, age four until I left for college. I actually hated it except when I was alone and could talk to my girl Goldie. It took me a long time to realize she was my only true friend back then." I smiled a little, thinking of my favorite horse when I was a child.

"And your safety isn't worth a little labor exchange?"

It was a good point, one I might have seen for myself if I wasn't still so shaken up by that guy, Farnsworth. "I don't know."

LOCKED

"Where will you go if you don't stay here?"

"Anywhere." There were still parts of the country I hadn't seen yet. "Maybe the Pacific Northwest."

"Too much rain and gray skies," she said dismissively. "Here is pretty good and I've been all over. This place just feels like home."

"That might have something to do with the fiancé I heard you have."

She laughed like a young girl. "True, but still, Opey is great. The guys are great, and Martha is an excellent cook."

Sounded like my old house. That thought pulled a wistful smile from me, making me wish I didn't miss my family so much. Wishing I could live up to Daddy's high expectations while also being happy. "You have a good life here."

"You don't want to stay? Fine. Stay and tell me about the tension between you and Holden. I'll feed you, so you're nice and nourished for your long drive to…anywhere."

"I don't know, Peaches. I don't want to intrude." This was Holden's space, and I was an uninvited visitor.

"You're not. Female companionship is hard to come by around here."

"My mama's been saying that since before I even knew what she meant. Ranch life is like that if you don't make friends with other ranch wives or women in town."

"This isn't your typical ranch, though."

"None of them are," I told her. "Several of my daddy's friends won their ranches in poker games. Or their granddaddies, sometimes great-granddaddies did too. There are land disputes that go back centuries and even a few Romeo & Juliet cases."

"No shit?"

"Ranching is more salacious than it seems," I told her, happy to be talking about something other than me and where I would lay my head tonight.

LOCKED

"Who knew?" Peaches laughed, a full-throated sound, filled with life and joy. "So, about you and Holden." Mischief sparkled in her eyes as she dropped her chin into her hand and waited.

I told her all about my unrequited crush on Holden, my bitchy rejection, and how much the man hated me today for those sins. "I deserve every bit of it," I told her honestly.

"People change. Lord knows everyone here has seen or done enough to make them see life a little differently." I wondered what she'd done or seen that had changed her outlook. "That's a story for if we become friends," Peaches said, somehow reading my mind. "You'd have to stay for that to happen."

"Real subtle, Peaches."

"The only thing subtle about me is my computer skills." She mimicked typing really fast, and I laughed. "Think about staying. Seriously."

"You don't give up." She filled the table with food while we talked. It was nice, spending the afternoon with another woman without competition over men or money or status. Or any of the other trivial shit women find to hate about each other. This was relaxing.

And by the time I had to pop the button on my jeans, I was thinking about staying at Hardtail Ranch forever.

At that thought, the back door smacked open and a man with a dark buzz cut and deep blue eyes that nearly matched Holden's walked in. He was tall and wide, imposing as all hell. "Babe, you in here?"

"Yep. Gettin' fat on Martha's biscuits. Want some?"

He grinned when his gaze found her. "Of you or the biscuits?"

"Both," she purred and wrapped her arms around him, accepting his kiss. "But there's someone I want you to meet first."

Uh oh. I stood and took one step back. Then another. And another. "Thanks for lunch and the uh, the dress Peaches."

LOCKED

"Hold it right there," she called out. For some damn reason, my feet stopped. "Aspen here is trying to get away from trouble from some guy named Farnsworth. He's looking for her ex. And she grew up on a ranch."

At those last words, his face lit up, and he finally looked at me. "A real ranch?"

"Ever heard of Wrangled Heart?"

"The beef?"

I nodded proudly. "That's my family's ranch, where I grew up."

I saw it, the moment he registered my connection to Holden. "Small world."

"It happens. Anyway, thanks again."

"Wait, do you need a place to stay?" he asked.

I shook my head. "Nah, I'll find a place as soon as I decide where to go." Having money made leaving in a hurry easy. And that's what I would use it for.

"Stay. Impart some of your ranch wisdom and lay low for a while."

That sounded good. Too good. Get lost in ranch work for a few weeks and forget about the past few years of my life. What could it hurt?

The answer came immediately. Holden.

"That sounds nice. If Holden is all right with it." This place would be no better, no safer than Ken's condo if Holden made my stay here miserable.

"He will be," she said immediately and with a certainty that just didn't feel possible.

I wasn't sure but then again, when in the hell had I ever been sure about anything? This would either be another giant mistake or a much smaller, insignificant mistake.

LOCKED

Chapter Thirteen

Holden

Back with my horses was where I belonged. The moment I walked into the stable, the smell of hay and horses and leather hit my nose. My shoulders relaxed, and little by little, as the morning wore on, I felt I was back to normal.

Unlike people, horses were simple. If I rubbed their necks and they liked it, they'd push me to keep doing it. If they were scared, they weren't shy about showing it. I preferred it that way, and I would trade favors with the other guys, if necessary, to get out of going back to The Barn Door. I appreciated the extra money in my pocket, but I could do without the drama.

And the people.

Shit. Spoke too soon.

Heavy-booted feet took slow, sure steps toward me, and I was pretty sure I knew who it was.

"We got a visitor," Gunnar said in his usual grumpy as hell tone.

I looked up at him, looking rougher than usual in a pair of black jeans and his shirt inside out.

"Another vet? I hear if you punch all the squares you get a VA discount." It was a lame joke, but I was sure the visitor wasn't on the ranch to see me, which meant I didn't understand what it had to do with me.

"Holden." There was something that struck me as odd about his tone, and when I looked up, sure enough, Gunnar's expression was bleak.

"What?" I stood so we were face-to-face so that he had to look me in the eye when he said whatever it was he came here to say. "Spit it out, Gunnar."

A look of surprise flashed across his face at my tone. For the most part, I was the easygoing guy of the bunch. Not much bothered me and my feathers didn't ruffle easily, or so the guys always said.

"Right. It's that woman, Aspen, the one you took care of the other night."

LOCKED

My shoulders stiffened at the mention of her name. "What about her? Why is she here?" But I knew. I already fucking knew. "No, Gunnar. Absolutely fucking not. No goddamn way, man."

It was one thing to invade the club a few nights while I happened to be there. But the ranch? This was my domain. My space. My home, goddammit.

"I wasn't asking." Arms folded so he looked even more like a fucking refrigerator, Gunnar wanted me to know who was boss.

Yeah, I fuckin' knew. "Dammit, man." This shit was no better than taking orders, and my feet began to move, to pace the length of the stables. Passing each horse and drawing their attention, I knew better than to let my emotions control me in front of the sensitive creatures. After a few more circuits, I stopped. Abruptly. And turned my gaze to the man in charge.

"Then I don't see why you bothered coming out here to let me know." I'd see her or I wouldn't.

He glared, unhappy with having to explain himself to me again, but this wasn't a goddamn monarchy. "Are you gonna question every goddamn thing I say?"

I shrugged. "I already told you once, Gunnar. I'm not putting my life on the line without explanation ever again." The first time was enough.

"Fine," he growled and reluctantly shared the details of Aspen's story, if it was even true. "He used the name Farnsworth, which didn't seem to mean anything to Aspen, but it did to Peaches." He paused and let the words sink in as if I could forget the trouble that showed up with her.

"She's pretty sure her trouble has cropped up again, and somehow Aspen's ex is connected to it."

His clear blue gaze was sober. Determined.

His mind was made up. Shit.

"Of course he is," I growled. "Still don't see what any of it has to do with me. She'll be here, and if I run into her, I'll do my best to be civil." That was all I could promise. All I was willing to promise.

Gunnar let out a resigned sigh, and I held my breath, waiting. "She's gonna help out on the ranch. Said she's good with horses, cattle, and crops. I figured you could use the help."

I had to snort at his words. "Good with? Her daddy has a spread in Vance nearly as big as all of Texas with a bank account to match, if that counts. But hey, you're in charge around here, right? You want her to help, then she helps."

I shrugged and turned back to Chaos, who was searching for the carrot I'd promised him earlier. I didn't need to see Gunnar when I could feel the hole he stared into the back of my head.

"What the fuck is your problem? All you do is give me shit lately."

"Nothing." It didn't matter what I thought, and like I said once before, I signed up for this shit. "She's gonna work with me. Fine. Anything else?"

His eyes were icy and angry, but I was beyond giving a shit. "Yeah, she's staying in the bunkhouse, and she's gonna need a horse while she's here. Think you can handle that?"

"Sure."

"Good. Her safety is now your responsibility." Message delivered, Gunnar turned and stomped his way out of the stables, and I leaned against the stable wall and blew out a breath.

Keeping Aspen Holt safe. Just fucking kill me now.

***

Being angry all the time tired me out. After a day filled with anger and frustration, I was fucking exhausted. Aspen hadn't shown her face by the end of the day, and I was damn happy about that. Still, the fact she was even on the ranch left me on edge. It was inevitable I'd see her, and there wasn't a fuckin' thing I could do to change it. No matter how much I tried to forget about it, to shove it out of my mind, it rattled around in my thoughts. Like a damn song I couldn't get out of my head.

That's why I sat out on the little porch that wrapped halfway around the cabin. I stared at the sky as the sun slowly sank behind the horizon, taking the last of the light with her. Usually, the beauty of this land was enough to calm me, but not this time, and it wasn't just the woman. It was the kind of trouble that was bound to follow.

As the last streaks of sun faded from the sky, a pair of long, denim-clad legs ate up the distance between us. A six-pack of beer in one hand and a flashlight in the other, she made a damn pretty sight. That fact alone made me want to be a dick to her, but I couldn't do anything about her presence on the ranch, yet, so I decided to play nice.

"You lost?"

She froze on the bottom step, and her big blue eyes connected with mine as a smile touched her lips.

"Nope. I brought a six-pack for us to share. Figured by the time the last bottle was empty maybe we could start over?"

It was an olive branch, and I was too damn tired to fight with her. "Sure. Come on up and take a seat."

"Thanks."

Her shoulders relaxed as she climbed the stairs and dropped down in the handmade rocking chair on the other side of the small barrel table. I'd set my first beer there. Maybe it was my second. Aspen positioned the six-pack on the table between us and pulled out a brown bottle, cracked it open, and took a long, fortifying pull.

"Thank you for trying to accept this." Her words sounded sincere, then again, women were excellent manipulators, and Aspen was better than most.

"I have accepted it, Aspen." Not that I was given much of a choice in the matter, but that wasn't her fault. No, that particular act of dumbassery was all mine. Work with her during the day and keep her safe at night. *Fucking Gunnar.* That's what I thought about the whole damn situation.

"I'm fine with it."

She laughed, but the sound wasn't light and feminine as I expected. Her words came out sharp and bitter and lacked all traces of amusement.

"You're not fine with it, and I get it."

She sighed as she stood with her beer in one hand and the flashlight in the other. "I'll do my best to stay out of your way," she said, sounding resigned to our arrangement. "Just leave a list of chores for me to do, and I'll take care of them."

"Playing the martyr now, Aspen?"

"No." I didn't think it was possible for her shoulders to fall lower, but somehow they did. "I don't want to make your life harder, Holden, and I know you don't have a reason to believe that, but it's true."

I did believe her, dammit, and that was part of the problem. I didn't want to believe Aspen, and I didn't want to like her. But I couldn't avoid her and keep her safe.

"Why did you come to Hardtail Ranch?"

At first, I thought maybe she wouldn't answer as she let her feet drop down one step and then the next until she stood in the dirt below and turned to face me.

"I came here to drop off the clothes your friend Peaches was nice enough to let me borrow. She fed me and got me talking, and somehow I ended up telling her things I shouldn't have." It looked like she regretted sharing her secret, which was something. "Contrary to the one bitchy thing I did to you all those years ago, I'm not here to disturb your peace, Holden."

Yeah, but she still managed to disturb it, but good. "Never thought you were. Just wondering how you got yourself mixed up with a guy like Ken. On the surface, he's exactly your type."

She let out a bitter laugh and dropped her butt down on the bottom step, as far from me as she could get, taking another long pull from her bottle. "It just took me a little longer than it should have for me to get below the surface."

That was an understatement. "How long?"

Her shoulders rose and fell, and she blew out a long, slow breath. "Way before the other day, if that's what you're asking. I knew after a while that something wasn't right, but I couldn't be sure what. You know how the horse and cattle businesses are, lots of shady characters."

Her golden hair, pulled into a low ponytail falling down her back, curled like a cat's tail as she shook her head in disgust. "I should have left sooner, but where would I go?"

"Back home, Aspen. Y'all aren't broke, are you?"

"No," she said and let out another bitter laugh that was so at odds with the woman on the surface. Even now she exuded elegance and sophistication in a simple outfit of jeans, a blue and white checked shirt, and worn cowboy boots. "That's the part I'm most humiliated about. I didn't stay with him because I needed him or because I loved him. I stayed because where else was I gonna go?"

"What's wrong with Vance?"

"And hear Daddy tell me 'I told you so' in about a million different ways every day for the rest of my life? No, thanks." She finished her beer and reached to slide it into the empty slot before looking up at me. "Don't worry, Holden, I'll get out of your hair as soon as possible."

Ah, hell. "Don't you worry about my hair, Aspen. It can take whatever you can dish out." When her gaze found mine, I let her see that I was amused by the situation, if also frustrated as hell by it.

"Really?" She got up as if to leave.

I gave a sharp nod and plucked two more beers from the pack, opening them both and handing her one. "Really. Take a load off and have a beer."

She grabbed the beer and held it up with a shaky smile. "To starting over."

LOCKED

What the hell? I lifted my bottle and tapped it to hers. "To starting over."

Chapter Fourteen

Aspen

My first day on the ranch started off the way I like it. With a big cup of black coffee and a piece of strudel Martha insisted I take with me when I left the big house about twenty minutes ago.

I quickly drained the coffee, but the hum in my blood remained, or maybe it was Holden showing me around the barn, looking mighty fine in a pair of faded and well-worn jeans that hugged the muscles of his thighs magnificently and cupped his ass fantastically. I tried to focus on his lecture, but his black shirt made him look like every bad boy cowboy fantasy I'd ever had as a teenage girl on a ranch full of cowboys. I couldn't take my eyes off his broad shoulders and wide chest that tapered down to a narrow waist.

Hot damn, but he made a fine specimen.

"And this beauty right here is Misfit," he said.

And he looked even hotter the way he smiled at the golden-brown mare who nuzzled his neck. "We just call her Lady because she's such a flirt."

"She's beautiful."

"She is." He said the words, but I heard the affection in his voice. "And she loves sugar cubes, but in a pinch, a carrot will do. Won't it, girl?" He was so sweet with her, gentle too. Proving that it was just me who brought out the asshole in Holden.

But he hadn't been an asshole last night. He'd accepted my peace offering and even let me sit and chat on my first night at the ranch. So I took a deep breath and stepped in close, letting Lady get familiar with me.

"Hey Lady, I'm Aspen. You're a pretty girl, aren't you?" I cooed and rubbed her nose, offering up the sugar cubes Holden had placed in my free hand. "Take it easy on me, girl. It's been awhile since I've been in the saddle."

"I remember when not a day passed that I wouldn't take my own horse, Goldie, out to roam the property. But that was a long time ago."

"Need a refresher course?" I heard the teasing in Holden's tone and glared up at him.

"No, Holden, I don't need a damn refresher on how to ride a horse." I snorted at the insinuation. "I've been riding longer than I've been walking." Which was the God's honest truth. "But it has been a while, and I'd like to ease into it, which should be easy because menial ranch chores don't require a horse." At least they hadn't when I was doing chores on Daddy's ranch. "Right?"

"Why would you assume that?"

Something about his tone changed and, alarmed, I took a step back.

"Maybe because you led Peaches and Gunnar to assume you've actually worked the land before?"

Oh, he was angry. Well, too damn bad. Because so was I.

I straightened my body to my full height, which was still nearly a foot shorter than Holden and got in his face. "Are you kidding me? I've been working horses and cattle since I was four years old. We were all expected to learn the ins and outs of the ranch if we were gonna live off Daddy's money."

One of Daddy's genius ideas that had produced some of the best times of my life. Of course, Holden didn't believe me. He didn't want to.

"My oldest sister, Sierra, she's the ranch manager. She'll get the biggest share when Daddy steps down, even though it kills him not to leave it to a man. Hell, Rosie and I, and even Pearl all learned the business. Rosie is a barrel racer, currently number two in the world."

Holden whistled, finally impressed, I suppose. "What about Pearl?"

"She's the rebel. Currently, in her second year of veterinary school."

LOCKED

And here I was, doing nothing with my life. Nothing to contribute to society and nothing to do with ranching, which was in my blood. "What happened to me, that's what you're thinking, isn't it?"

Holden shrugged, for once too polite to say what was really on his mind.

"Daddy wanted me to marry the son of a business associate to create an empire, or so he said. The guy was a world class creep, and I refused. After that, Daddy pretty much washed his hands of me."

Thinking about it—never mind talking about it—hurt like hell. But Holden needed to know. "He wouldn't let me help out on the ranch and stopped inviting me to dinners at the country club with the family. He pushed me out until my only option was to leave."

I hated to think of how easy it was for my own father to basically boot me out of the family for choosing my own path, but the hurt had lessened with time. It had scabbed over and only ached when it was picked at, like now.

"Well, he's a goddamn idiot because I never turn down help. But the so-called *menial* ranch chores, for now, are going to the prospect, Ford, over there." He nodded to the beefy blond with the babyface who was carrying a saddle right toward us.

"A prospect? Is that like an intern or something?"

His lips twitched, telling me I'd gotten it all wrong, but he didn't bother to explain. "Long story," he said, and I watched his big body amble off, meeting Ford at the halfway point between them. Holden was a big man who moved with the capable grace of a dancer, but he definitely held himself like a soldier. A cowboy.

I wanted so bad to learn about the man he was today, but it was pointless. He tolerated me now because he had to, and that was fine. I'd finally learned my lesson about sticking around where I wasn't wanted.

Holden finished with the prospect and walked back to me, carrying the saddle as if it weighed nothing. "Remember how to saddle a horse?"

LOCKED

I glared at him again and snatched the saddle from him, nearly toppling over at the weight of it, but a pair of big strong hands grabbed my waist before I hit the ground. "Thanks," I mumbled and pulled out of his grasp, ignoring his barely suppressed laughter. "You used to be a lot nicer, you know."

He laughed, but instead of bitter, the sound was almost wistful. "Yeah, well you used to be the girl of my dreams."

It was impossible to explain how much Holden's words stung me because I didn't even know he had any words that could hurt me so much. But there they were, the dirty truth of the matter. I used to be that girl, the one that inspired men like Holden to believe I was some fantasy woman. Some prize to be had. And it was all the more hurtful knowing I was no longer that girl. Now I was nothing. I was nobody with no place to go.

Maybe Peaches was right and here with the misfits was exactly where I belonged.

KB WINTERS

Chapter Fifteen

Holden

Ranch work meant long hard days, and my second full day working side by side with Aspen was exhausting as hell. She knew ranch work, a lot actually, but dammit, she smelled too good, and her jeans were too damn tight. It was hard to concentrate on the tasks at hand and believe me the list never seemed to get shorter.

After a quick, hot shower, I found myself standing in front of an empty fridge and willing it to have something in it. I would have taken week-old pizza or a leftover casserole Martha handed off on one of my visits to the big house. But no, there wasn't a goddamn thing but an almost empty carton of milk and an unopened package of cheese.

Which meant that I was headed over to the big house for dinner. Again. As soon as I stepped inside the spacious, colorful space, I was set upon by a three-foot-tall munchkin.

"Holden, I missed you!" Maisie ran full speed in my direction, not stopping until her little body collided with mine and she had wrapped her arms tight around my legs.

It was a welcome greeting even from a kid who'd address the Easter Bunny the same way. It didn't stop me from lifting her in my arms and holding her tight before I smacked a loud kiss on her rosy cheeks.

"Hey kiddo, I missed you, too. You haven't been working the ranch like I expected." She giggled when I poked her little belly, holding me tight as she let go, laughing with wild abandon. "I sure hope you saved me some dinner."

"Nope," she laughed. "We didn't eat yet cuz Martha says Gunny moves like he has molasses in his ass."

LOCKED

Laughter exploded from me at her unexpected words, even though I knew I faced the wrath of whatever adults lingered in the kitchen. Out of view.

"Maisie, watch your mouth!" Peaches' loud voice boomed from the kitchen, but we could even hear her laughter from the living room.

"Sorry," the kid said, not looking sorry at all.

"And you, Holden, you're no better than her," she shouted back, startled when we appeared in the doorway. "A bunch of kids, the whole damn lot of you."

"You love it," I told her with a wink. Other than Martha, no woman could command the guys better. "Where's lover boy?"

At that moment the front door opened and smacked closed, followed by two sets of footsteps. One was unmistakably Gunnar's. The other, Aspen. Both of them wore worried expressions that immediately put me on edge.

"What?" I said, waiting for either of them to answer.

"Nothing," Aspen insisted, keeping her gaze down as she took the seat beside Peaches.

Fine, she didn't want to tell me, she didn't have to. I turned to Gunnar. "Well?"

"Ken's been blowing up her phone. Twenty calls and forty text messages since this morning. Non-fucking-stop."

Shit. This guy had decided to go crazed stalker route instead of just giving up gracefully. "So what are the calls? Does he want to get back together or what?" My gaze fell to Aspen, looking pale and terrified, which meant she knew more than she was letting on.

She sighed, taking the small tumbler of whiskey Martha helpfully put in her hands. "It'll settle your nerves girl, drink up. This is no time to worry about calories."

"Thanks," Aspen whispered, but even that was barely audible as Martha made a ton of noise, shuffling out the back door, leaving us all alone. Finally.

LOCKED

"He says he wants to get back together, but believe me, Ken has never been that invested in us. Plus, he's frantic about getting back together, about me calling him back like it's something else." Aspen shook her head again, damp blonde hair falling all around her shoulders. "I don't know." She sounded scared. Genuinely scared.

"What could it be then?" I felt a tug on my collar and looked down into Maisie's concerned blue eyes, realizing this was not the time or place for this conversation.

"Later. We'll talk more later because little Maisie promised me dinner." I tickled her again, letting the sound of her laughter ease the tension from the kitchen.

Dinner was a mostly silent affair, more so now that most of the guys ate someplace else, mostly to give Gunnar and Peaches alone time, but also to avoid the viper twins. I sucked down two and a half helpings of Martha's roast, mashed potatoes, and roasted vegetables, not to mention three biscuits topped with gravy. It was the best thing about ranch work. It burned a shit ton of calories, which meant there was always room for Martha's delicious meals.

As always, after one of the cook's feasts, I needed a cold beer and some fresh air. The land was now drenched in darkness, but I still marveled at the beauty of it. I'd stood on this porch with two previous owners, talking ranch business mostly. Now, conversations were a little different.

The door smacked shut when Gunnar stepped out to join me. "You getting the feeling this, the brothers from before and now Ken, is all somehow related?"

"The thought had crossed my mind. What are the odds that all this shit has come to this little town in Texas and it's not all related?"

"Pretty fucking slim," he grunted out before taking a long pull of his beer. "Peaches thinks it all comes back to Farnsworth."

Shit. "Isn't that guy dead?" This shit was starting to make my head spin.

"Yeah, but it's a name they all use, like a goddamn factory that keeps creating the same person over and over. He never dies, which makes him terrifying, or so I'm told." Gunnar didn't sound any happier about it than I felt, which provided some comfort.

"How do you think Ken is mixed up in all this?" Because Farnsworth was a problem that wouldn't go away, we needed to know how far this guy was willing to go to get to Peaches. "And do you think we can trust Aspen?"

Gunnar laughed. "Shouldn't I be asking you that question?"

"No. Haven't known her since she was a girl, and even then, she wasn't the girl I thought she was." That was as much of an explanation as I planned to give. "She seems genuinely afraid, but she could just be a good actress."

"Yeah, I've thought about that, but unless she's a psychopath, I don't think this is the kind of excitement she's after. And she has her own money."

A fact Ken had to have known. "Why do you think he didn't go after her money?"

"Maybe she doesn't have access to it yet. You said she was a rich girl. Don't they have trust funds and shit?"

"Yeah, but she's over twenty-one. She has to have access to it by now." And the fact that he hadn't touched it was bothering the shit out of me. "Doesn't make sense."

"I don't think I was—or am—part of the plan."

Aspen's voice sounded from the door. Gunnar and I both turned to face Peaches and Aspen.

"You're right," she said. Those blue eyes seared me, filled with disappointment and embarrassment and fear, and they never looked away. "I always wondered why Ken never asked for money, even when his gambling got out of hand or he forgot to pay someone back. I wondered, but never asked why he paid for the condo outright when I just as easily could have. For a while I thought it was love."

LOCKED

Her last words were clipped and bitter.

"And now what do you think?"

"Holden," Peaches admonished and put a protective hand on Aspen's shoulder.

"No, it's all right. I think he's an asshole."

Gunnar frowned and opened the door, forcing the women back. I followed them all back to the table. "How long have you been in Opey?"

She shrugged. "About nine, maybe ten months. I met Ken about an hour from here, that roadside diner with all the Dallas Cowboys memorabilia? Both of us suffered tire fatalities from the same stretch of road and commiserated while the guy overcharged us both for the privilege."

"And?"

She blinked at my tone and offered up an apologetic smile. "My car didn't get fixed. We spent the night together. That was about a year ago, give or take a few months." It was clear she had more to say, so I kept my mouth shut for once. "We were living in San

Antonio, and then out of the blue he wanted to move to Opey for a job opportunity, but he never said what it was."

Gunnar leaned forward, trying to be patient and gentle even though he had to be as frustrated as I was about the slow trickle of information. "You said he gambled and had debts? Any idea who he owes?"

She shook her head and gave another shrug. "No. Honestly, I never bothered myself with the details because I didn't care since I didn't need his money. But I've been thinking. It would have been weird for a guy like him to move to a town like this on his own. He would have stood out." She directed the words at me since we both grew up in a small town where there were no secrets and no strangers.

"You're right."

Her shoulders relaxed. "Plus your, uh, club. Having a partner helps or so I'm told."

LOCKED

Ah, shit. Now I would have to tell her the truth. "He's been to the club before. Ford said he's been a regular for months."

She barked out a bitter laugh. "I'm not actually surprised, but I have no idea who that woman was he was with...last time."

Peaches stood unceremoniously and ran up the stairs, returning a minute later with one of her laptops.

"Okay, Aspen, you spit those details back at me, and we'll see what I can find. You boys go talk or plot or whatever." She flashed a sweet smile at Gunnar. "Love you, babe."

Gunnar and I took the hint, this time grabbing our beers and heading to the front porch. "If he's in debt, anyone could have bought it." Frustration radiated off his broad shoulders.

"Including this Farnsworth asshole."

"Feels like we're already thick in the shit, and we haven't even ID'd what kind of shit it is yet."

The man definitely had a way with words, and I clapped him on the back and told him as much. "It's shit. Does the kind really matter? We gotta flush it, bury it, or burn it, Prez."

Gunnar's lips twitched, and he punched my shoulder.

"Now he remembers." It was a moment of forgiveness between men. No words were needed. We'd forgotten all the shit from the past few weeks in the face of something bigger than us. His smile faded along with mine.

"We need to figure out what Ken has to do with this. And Aspen, and sooner rather than fucking later."

"Got it." I knew what I had to do. Get close to Aspen to get all the details I could. The Reckless Bastards needed me to come through, and I wouldn't fuck it up.

Chapter Sixteen

Aspen

"Aspen, babe, call me back. Look I know you're pissed, but I really need to talk to you."

I ended and deleted that message quickly. I didn't want to hear anything Ken had to say. I wasn't heartbroken, either. I was angry. So angry with myself that I'd wasted so much time on a man who clearly had never been into me. Beyond the sex, anyway.

A whole fucking year wasted on a man not worth more than one night. I was determined that I wouldn't waste another minute on him, but his nonstop calls made it difficult.

A knock sounded on the bunkhouse door, which was weird. No one ever knocked. Not even the other guys who never seemed appropriately apologetic about it, either.

"Come in."

Seconds later, Holden made his appearance, looking good enough to eat in his standard jeans and t-shirt, except today everything was clean and with significantly fewer holes. Too bad, because those little peeks of skin helped make the long hot days on the ranch bearable.

"Sorry to bother you so early." He looked nervous, which honestly, was a little bit shocking.

"That's all right. Am I late for something?"

At my question, Holden's broad shoulders squared. "No," he said, and he stood a little taller. "I thought maybe you might want some help to pick up the rest of your things from Ken's place."

"You did?" It didn't make sense. Sure things with Holden were now civil, but he'd shown no signs over the past week that he was ready to be friendly, never mind friends.

"Why?"

LOCKED

He shrugged. "Maybe if he sees you've replaced him with someone who can kick his ass, he'll leave you alone."

I didn't believe him, not at all, but it would be nice to have a pair of strong arms to help me carry my stuff. Something was going on around here, and I didn't know what, but I was starting to notice a few things. Like the way Peaches reacted to the name Farnsworth and all the questions they had about Ken. I needed to be careful and wary.

"Sure," I said and followed him to the plot of land outside used as a parking lot. I watched the dusty miles roll by, lost in my own thoughts until we pulled into town.

"You ready to see him if he's there?" Holden's deep drawl cut through the silence in the truck as he shifted into park and killed the engine.

"No, but I'm a big girl, and I can handle it."

He nodded, accepting my answer, but at the end of the day, Holden was still a man. "Want me to come in with you?"

"No. That'll only make things worse if he's there." I had to do this on my own. Ken was my choice and my mess, and I would clean it up myself. With Holden in the pickup for backup if necessary.

Luckily, Ken wasn't home, but the place did look ransacked, so I left the door open and crept inside, going straight for the bedroom closet where I'd stored my suitcases. I laid two Louis Vuitton bags open on the bed and filled them faster than I'd ever packed, throwing in whatever I could find because this would be my last trip to this address. When I left it behind this time, I was gone forever. Packing in twenty minutes had to be a record for me. It was odd that no one around to pat me on the back for my achievement, so I did it myself.

Looking at the condo now, I realized that this place had never been my home. It was a place I slept in and where I passed the time, but I hadn't done any actual living in here. I hadn't made my mark. I hadn't turned it into a home. I pulled the big suitcase along behind me and hefted the duffel over my forearm before dropping the key into the little plate Ken never used.

With one last look, I stepped outside and ran right into the man I'd very nearly avoided. He tried to block my exit, but I used the weight of my suitcase to put some distance between us.

"Aspen," he frowned. "Where do you think you're going?"

"Exactly where I've been, Ken. Away from here. Away from you."

He laughed. "Yeah, and where are you gonna go? I know for a fact your daddy won't have you."

It was a low blow, but luckily, I didn't give a damn what Ken thought anymore. "I don't need him. Or you."

"Since when?"

"Since I realized you're both selfish pieces of shit who don't care about anyone but yourselves. Why do you even care, Ken? You don't want me."

I leaned in, noticing the telltale signs of exhaustion on his face, the red lines in his eyes that said he was high or drunk. Probably both.

"Maybe I need you," he slurred, but I didn't miss the emphasis. "To make some shit right."

"It's a good thing I wasn't expecting romance. Make what right, Ken?" If I had him here, I might as well get some useful information. Earn my stay on Hardtail Ranch for as long as I planned to be there.

"Everything," he slurred again, this time his words were strained and filled with fear or doubt. I didn't know Ken was capable of either of those emotions. His legs swayed again, and then he remembered his anger.

"You're not going anywhere. I need you." He reached for me, and I took a step back, earning a dark look for my efforts. "Don't run from me, Aspen. You're nothing without me."

I laughed at his pitiful attempt at tearing me down. "Get your fucking hands off me!" I snarled.

He was angry and on something, and I really didn't want to fight with him, but there was no reasoning with him when he was like this.

"Damn you, Ken." I pulled my leg back and let my knee loose right between his legs.

"Bitch," he growled and wrapped a hand around my wrist to steady himself as he stood straight. "You're not going anywhere. I need you." I reared my leg back again, and he twisted my arm.

"Ow!"

Then Ken's hand was gone, and he flew back against the white siding of the condo, feet dangling about two feet in the air with Holden's hand the only thing keeping him from falling.

"I believe she said to get your fuckin' hands off her." Holden was a big man, who seemed even bigger by Ken's small stature. Or, maybe it was the way he held him by the throat so easily. So effortlessly.

"You get off on manhandling women?"

"My. Woman." He managed to choke the words out, hoping for what, I didn't know.

Just in case. "Ex," I added because it felt like an important point to make. "Ex-woman."

"Don't be stupid, Aspen." He glared at me, a threat forming in his brown eyes. "I'll find you. Ow!" he said, bending into his gut. Holden had twisted his arm down until he faced his shoes. "What the fuck was that for?"

"Don't threaten her." Holden was as cheap with his threats as he was with his words.

Ken's eyes went wide and then a smile formed on his lips, earning him a tighter squeeze from Holden. "You're fucking a cowboy now? Oh, how the princess has fallen," he laughed. No, it was more like a sneer.

LOCKED

I shrugged. "Better a cowboy than a half-ass criminal who can't control his gambling or his teeny tiny cock."

I shook my head at the pathetic picture he made, in a position of weakness but still issuing threats. That was what my Daddy would call a first-class idiot.

"Oh, and your friend Farnsworth showed up while you were off getting herpes. He threatened me and put his hands on me, not that you give a damn."

"Farnsworth? Are you sure that's what he said?" That was panic, pure and simple. "What else did he say?"

"I don't know Ken, and I don't give a fuck. Whatever you've gotten yourself into, deal with it on your own. Or maybe the newest, flavor to warm your bed." With those words, Holden released him. It was immensely satisfying to see him fall to the concrete in a heap.

Holden grabbed the large suitcase and left without another word.

"You'll regret this, bitch! I promise."

I laughed at the pathetic picture he made. "The same way you promised we'd see the world? That I'd come harder than I ever had in my life? Add it to all the other promises I'm waiting on you to fulfill, dickhead."

I walked away from Ken feeling good, feeling better about myself. About my situation. No wonder Rosie never took shit from anyone. It felt damn good to tell an asshole where to shove it.

Chapter Seventeen

Holden

"I don't want you going anywhere without telling me, especially leaving the ranch."

Dammit, I thought Gunnar was just trying to punish me. I didn't think Aspen was actually in danger. I thought she was making it all up for attention.

"What?" She turned to me, outrage turning her cheeks pink. "I don't think so. You're not the boss of me, Holden."

"Goddamn right I'm not, because if I were, I'd just chain your sweet little ass to the nearest bed to make sure you stay safe. And you're not safe, just in case that little fact slipped your mind."

She laughed. She actually fucking threw her head back and laughed. "Oh please. Ken is no more dangerous than a fly."

Her dismissiveness pissed me off. "You may not think he poses a danger, but Ken is an addict, Aspen.

Everything he does serves one purpose, to feed his addiction. Don't think for one second he wouldn't try to hold you for ransom or kidnap you and keep you while he drains your trust fund if he needed it. He would." And I was sure the bastard had thought of it, after seeing him in action.

"And I don't have to worry about that with you?" I heard the skepticism in her tone, and yeah, it pissed me off until I reminded myself she was smart to be suspicious.

"Sweetheart, I don't want a damn thing from you."

"You've made that quite clear," she grumbled, and it was so adorable, the way she folded her arms and stuck out her bottom lip.

I couldn't help but laugh. "Is that why you're so bent out of shape? You're butt hurt that I'm not drooling over you like I used to?" It was mean to laugh at her, I knew that, but damn this woman. "Does your ego have no limits?"

LOCKED

A low growl escaped, and I risked a glance to my side, seeing her red-faced with her nostrils flaring. "It's not about being butt hurt, you asshole. I am a person. A goddamn flesh and blood human being, not a cushion for you to poke when the mood strikes and certainly not a punching bag for your amusement!"

She had a point, but I wasn't ready to concede for a variety of reasons, the most important being how sexy she looked all riled up and angry. "You mean like accusing the man who's trying to help you of trying to access your precious trust fund?" She didn't say anything, and I shook my head, returning my gaze to the road. "You can dish it out, but you can't take it."

"Oh I can take it all right," she insisted, notching her chin up defiantly. "But you are an asshole, Holden Jennings."

"Never claimed I wasn't, Aspen Holt." I was an asshole who was more used to horses and guns than people but sparring with her was more fun than I'd had all month. Hell, all year. "If it makes you feel better, I still think you're a looker."

"It doesn't," she insisted haughtily, but I saw the pink rise up her chest and throat before it took over her face.

"It does. It's okay to feel good that even someone like me enjoys looking at you, princess. I won't bite." Not unless she asked, no begged, me to.

"Screw you! I grew up with someone like you, hundreds of them. Including you!" She punched me in the shoulder to bring her point home, and I stilled.

"Aspen," I warned.

"No. You want to keep punching at me, maybe I'll do the same," she said and sent alternating punches into my right arm. "Doesn't feel too good, does it?" Again and again, she punched me in my right shoulder until I couldn't take it anymore, pulling the truck over about a half-mile from home.

"Dammit, woman, stop hitting me."

She punched me again.

"Aspen."

LOCKED

She did it again and laughed.

I grabbed her wrist, and she gasped. "You're playing with fire, girl." I let her look into my eyes, long and hard, so she understood just what she was doing. How close I was to losing control and doing something I'd only ever dreamed of doing with her.

"Maybe I want to." Her words were a whisper, but I heard a certainty in them I desperately wanted to be true.

She didn't. Couldn't. "You don't. I'm not offering you anything but a fuck, Aspen."

She rolled her eyes. "Like I'd want any more than that when you're the world's biggest dick."

I grinned. "You've heard the stories, then?"

Aspen scoffed and rolled her eyes, for just a second looking like the sweet, beautiful girl I'd watched for four years turn into a stunning woman. "I've heard about your dick before."

"I'm sure you have," I told her and slid over, so the steering wheel was no longer in the way. "But I just want to make sure there are no misunderstandings."

"There aren't," she whispered with a smile I couldn't resist, so I didn't bother. I grabbed her by the back of the head and slammed my mouth against hers. The kiss wasn't elegant or romantic; it was intense and raw and hungry. And when her tongue slicked out, touched mine, I growled into her and pulled her onto my lap.

"Aspen." My lips moved from her mouth to her long, sweet neck, kissing and licking while she ground against my cock, making him harder and harder.

"Holden," she groaned, "Fuck, it's fucking huge." She arched into me as desire took over her body.

It was fast and frantic. I yanked her shirt up and over her head, revealing the gorgeous swell of pale tits and sweet raspberry nipples. "Delicious," I whispered and pulled one into my mouth, sucking and tasting it before moving on.

LOCKED

"Yes."

Aspen arched into me, speared her fingers through my hair to hold me closer, while I brought her closer and closer to the edge with nothing more than my tongue on her nipples. "So fucking sweet."

"Holden, please." She fought to get off my lap, and I froze for a second, wondering if I'd done something wrong. Hoping like hell I wouldn't have to take care of this boner inside the walls of a cold fucking shower.

"What?" She rolled off to the side, grunting as she worked her pants free before stopping to look at me. "Why aren't you taking off your pants?"

She didn't have to ask me twice. I flipped open my button and tugged on my zipper, shoving my jeans and boxers down as far as I could without leaving her side. "Better?"

Wide blue eyes stared at my cock, making me grow harder by the fucking second. Aspen swallowed. "Holy shit, you weren't joking. That thing is massive."

I laughed at her words even though she sounded more scared than up for the challenge. "Scared?"

"Any smart woman would be," she said and finally kicked off her jeans and pink panties. "But I find myself dangerously intrigued," she said and kicked one leg over my hips until her wet pussy lips opened around the ridge of my cock, releasing the scent of her arousal and coating my cock in it. "Go slow."

My hands held her hips as she slid back and forth over the length of me until my cock glistened with her juices. "You go slow, Aspen." I kept my hands where they were, letting her decide how to proceed. Even if it fucking killed me.

"I want to see that monster cock up close. I want to taste it and see if I can get you to crack, but right now I just want you inside of me. Fucking me. Please, Holden."

I stroked my cock, mesmerizing her until she licked her lips and sighed, grabbing my cock until it was lined up with the sweet nectar that dripped from her pussy and sliding down. Slowly.

LOCKED

"Oh, fuck!" She was so goddamn tight and hot and wet, my cock pulsed and twitched inside of her. "Shit, Aspen."

"Fuck, so big. Slow."

"It's all you, babe."

She grinned, slowly bouncing on my cock until inch by inch I was fully seated inside her dripping cunt. "Oh, wow. Oh, fuck me, wow!" It took Aspen no time to adjust to my size, her greedy pussy taking me deeper and deeper, pulsing around me and coating me in cream.

She was a wildcat, bouncing on my cock like it was her favorite carnival ride, screaming and growling and making all kinds of noises that society wouldn't deem appropriate, but I found erotic as fuck. Clenching around my cock, I knew she was close, and I leaned forward, taking a sweet nipple one more time with a growl.

"Fuck. Oh, fuck, yes! Yeah, Holden. Oh. Fuck. Yes." The last word was barely a whisper as she collapsed on my chest, her body still twitching and convulsing as her orgasm worked its way free.

But I wasn't there, not yet. Even as she folded herself limp against me, I gripped her hips tight and thrust up into her, hard and fast, chasing my own orgasm in the confines of her still pulsing pussy.

"Aspen," I hissed. She sat up and leaned back, planting her elbows on the dashboard for an angle that sent us both over the edge in seconds.

"Oh, fuck! Shiiiit!" My hips jerked and twitched, right there in the front seat of my truck as I shot my load into Aspen fucking Holt.

It was a mistake, and I should have been filled with regret but with her cunt still wrapped around me, little aftershocks squeezing the last of my jizz out of me, I couldn't find regret anywhere.

"Wow." Her voice filled with awe.

Yeah, that about summed it up.

Chapter Eighteen

Aspen

"Don't think this means that I'm gonna do what you tell me to, 'cause I won't." Though if Holden didn't stop running his fingertips up and down the length of my spine, he might make a liar out of me.

"Yeah?" He leaned in close, the deep rumble of his voice making me shiver. "And if I told you to lie back on the bed and spread your legs so I can feast on you again?"

I didn't lie back because I had a point to make, but slowly I spread my legs to let him know what I thought of the command.

"I'd say feast away. But we're aren't talking about that." Hell, I didn't know why we were talking about anything at all when he was naked, and I was naked, and we were all alone in his cabin.

Naked.

"No. We're talking about your safety."

"My safety is not an issue. Even if it were, it's not your issue!" This was the strangest conversation to have while we were naked and sweaty, bodies barely disentangled.

"Yeah well, I'm making it my issue, dammit. You need someone to look after you, and since you clearly prefer to underestimate your ex, it'll have to be me." Holden sat up straight and turned to face me. All I could do was stare at his expansive chest, his skin, and the dark hair that made it look even paler.

"What do you care? You don't even like me." Was that an echo or déjà vu, because I could've sworn I'd had this conversation already with another man.

"I like you just fine, more so now." His lips curled into a seductive smile that made my nipples tighten and my belly clench. Hard. "And just because I don't think you hang the moon like I used to, doesn't mean I want something to happen to ya."

"Wait, you used to think I hung the moon. Me?"

He nodded and swung his long legs off the side of the bed. "Yep. The way you would compliment Mary Beth Higgins' clothes even though they never fit quite right and were out of style."

I can't believe he remembered that. "She was always nice to me. Tutored me in geometry and always had notes when I missed class. God, I haven't thought about her in ages."

"Maybe not," he said gruffly. "But I'll bet the kindness you showed her made her memories of high school a lot less miserable."

"Too bad I couldn't do the same for you." I hated that memory was there between us, making it hard to move forward.

"My memories are just fine, Aspen. You were cruel that day, but you taught me a valuable lesson."

"Never pine for a spoiled rich girl?"

He turned, and his lips kicked into an amused grin. "That, too," he said, ominously, without ever really answering the question. "Look, I don't hate you, and I want to keep you safe from whatever the hell is going on with you and your ex. Don't argue with me about it." He turned and disappeared into the bathroom as if that were the end of the conversation.

"Excuse me?" I jumped off the bed, not giving a damn about my naked state and marched into the bathroom. "Do you hear the shit that comes out of your mouth?"

He stood in front of the mirror, brushing his teeth. He spat and stared at me in the mirror. "I'm not the one with the hearing problem. Does 'you'll regret this bitch' sound familiar to you?"

It wasn't fair, the way he flung Ken's words at me like that. "It was just talk."

"It always is. 'Til it isn't." His blue gaze, even through the filter of the mirror, sent a shiver through me and not of the sexual variety. "Whatever you think of me, Aspen, I don't want to control you. As long as you're on Hardtail, we're all responsible for you. Including me."

LOCKED

"I don't want to be anyone else's responsibility, Holden."

He had the nerve to laugh at me. "Life is full of responsibilities, Aspen. It's called helping out your fellow man. Maybe try it some time."

He was such a jerk. How could I have slept with him and enjoyed it so damn much? His big damn cock left me dickmatized, that was the only thing that made sense. That and my long history of making appallingly bad choices when it came to men. "This coming from a biker-slash-cowboy?"

"This biker-slash-cowboy saved your ass from a beating earlier." Even as he said the words, Holden's nostrils flared, and his free hand flexed in anger. "Don't forget that."

"I won't. Ever." He had saved me. Ken had never raised a hand to me before, which only confirmed that I was right to leave.

"A biker gang, really? How'd that happen?" It didn't sound like the boy I remembered, then again I never would've imagined Holden was packing a python in his pants.

"A motorcycle club," he clarified with a shrug. "Same way any other club forms, I suppose. We're all vets so I guess you could say we just went from one club to another."

"Now I feel like a jerk, thanks."

His deep burst of laughter startled me, but when my eyes set on him, I couldn't look away. Holden was a good-looking man, look up sexy as hell cowboy in the dictionary, and his brooding picture complete with ass hugging denim and big ol' Stetson would be there. But hot damn when he smiled, it made me melt. "You're welcome."

"It wasn't that funny."

"Funny is funny," he said with a shrug and put his toothbrush into the deep blue holder on the sink. His gaze turned predatory, and I had a feeling our conversation was coming to an end. "So, do we have this all settled now? You'll let me know where you are?"

LOCKED

"Nope." I couldn't give up control of my life like that to anyone. Ever.

"And here I thought you were gonna do things the easy way for once." Before I could ask him what the hell he was going on about, Holden grabbed me by the waist and picked me up, setting me down on the edge of the bathroom vanity.

"I wasn't even born the easy way," I told him, recounting one of Daddy's favorite stories. "Made my mama get all the way dilated before turning around and trying to go back, so they had to cut me out." I flashed a smile, but Holden didn't share it.

"Aspen?"

"Yeah," I answered, breathless from his proximity.

"Don't be nervous. This ain't gonna hurt a bit." His lips curled into a seductive grin as he leaned in and nipped my ear. His hips parted my legs, and Holden fitted himself between them like he belonged there.

Then one long, blunt finger slid between my pussy lips, making me gasp.

"Who's nervous?" I was turned on as hell. Breathless. Ready to burst. But not nervous.

"Good point. Now," he leaned back and looked at me, letting his gaze travel the length of my body and back up again, like a caress. "Let's talk about your safety."

"Now? Are you…ah!" That same finger slid all the way inside and my body wrapped around it greedily.

"Yeah, now is as good a time as any, wouldn't you say?" Damn that teasing smile that had my pussy clamping down on his finger. "So turned on, so fucking wet already. Good." He was teasing me. Torturing me to get me to do his bidding. Dammit. "You'll tell me where you are?"

I shook my head, prepped my lips to say now when another finger joined the first. "Oh, God!"

"Not God, just Holden." Amusement rang in his voice, so close to my ear that his warm breath was as effective as the two fingers sliding in and out of me in a lazy rhythm that made me crazy. "You'll let me know where you are so that I can keep you safe."

"Holden." I couldn't focus on his words, not when his deep rumbling voice was like another hand gliding over my skin and not when his thumb started slow, inconsistent circles on my clit.

"You'll let me keep you safe," he said and thrust into me again, tapping his fingers to hit the spot that sent fireworks shooting off behind my eyelids. "Because you owe me." When my eyes slammed open, Holden wore a big-ass, satisfied smile.

"Really? I'd say you're the one who owes me."

"Yeah, you would say that." How the hell the man could talk when his fingers were buried so deep inside me, I couldn't say. All I could do was feel the way his fingers thrust in and out, the way his thumb grew more and more eager around my clit. And good God, the way his gaze ate me up like I was sweet tea on a sweltering Texas day. "Say yes, Aspen."

"No." I frowned up at him when his hands stilled. "Why'd you stop?"

"I'm not hearing what I want to hear."

Goddamn pussy tease is what he is. "Holden."

"Aspen." He sighed and vigorously tapped that spot again. "I just want to keep you safe. I'm not telling you where to go or what to do, but knowing where you are will help us all keep you safe."

I didn't like the idea that I needed to be kept safe. But I knew for a fact that my body would explode in three...two... "Fiiine." I grabbed his wrist and swirled my hips in fast, greedy circles. He dipped down and sucked my pussy when the juices started flowing, and for a few seconds, I forgot who the fuck I was.

***

"Jalapenos on pizza, Aspen? And here I thought you were cool." Peaches shook her head at the slice that sat beside a salad on my plate.

LOCKED

"What can I say? I prefer my pizza with a bit of spice." And this small Texas town had damn good pizza and fresh jalapenos. "Besides, someone who eats broccoli on pizza has no room to talk."

Maisie snickered from her spot beside Peaches in the booth we shared. "Can I go play games, Peaches?"

"Sure." She dug out a few quarters and stood to let Maisie out of the booth. She knelt in front of her before handing her the change. "Stay where I can see you."

Maisie pouted, but she gave an obedient nod before throwing her arms around Peaches with a wide smile. "I will. Thank you!"

Peaches shook her head as she slid back inside the booth. "That girl has more energy in her thumb than I can muster up in a week." She turned her gaze back to me. "And broccoli and sausage is the perfect pizza, objectively speaking."

"I'll take your word for it, Peaches." There was something about this woman that I liked. She was brash and loud and didn't let other people's opinions and expectations bother her, which I kind of respected. The fact that she was nice and somehow seemed to wrangle half a dozen bikers was impressive as hell. "So how did you get into computer stuff?"

She huffed out a laugh and finished chewing before she answered. "Tons of foster homes with internet and no supervision. I picked it up quickly and then got in some trouble that gave me access to a steady stream of jobs." Peaches blew out a long, stressed breath that sent a few strands of curls flying high above her head. "And those jobs are the source of my current troubles. And yours, possibly."

I blinked a few times until her words sank in. Her tone and the serious look on her face made me feel like an ass for giving Holden so much shit earlier. "What do you mean?"

Peaches gave me a strange look. Head cocked to the side and hazel eyes mentally calculating, what I had no idea, only that she was sizing me up and not in the female against female kind of way. "I'm trying to decide if I should tell you, Aspen."

LOCKED

I huffed out a laugh. "I'm still trying to learn how to trust myself, so I can't help ya there."

"Fair enough." She nodded and pushed those wild curls out of her face. "Gunnar doesn't think I should share this with you until we know for sure you are well and truly done with your ex, so let's start there. Are you even considering going back to him?" Her tone held no judgment, so I relaxed against the booth; my answer came firmly.

"Hell, no." I didn't know whether I could trust Peaches or Gunnar or even Holden, but they were offering help when no one else was, so I decided to go with honesty for once. "Things have been bad for a while, and I was just complacent, I guess. But whatever Ken is into, it's bad, like dangerous bad, and that combined with everything else means we're done for good."

Satisfied with that answer, Peaches nodded and held up a finger in the universal sign for 'wait' as Maisie ran back to the table for more quarters and a bite of pizza. "Thanks. Love you," she said and darted off once more.

I envied the look Peaches sent the little girl. It was obvious they loved each other very much and were a real family. But I couldn't dwell on what I didn't have, not now. "What don't I know, besides everything?"

She flashed a sympathetic look and took a sip of the peach tea in her tall red cup.

"Ken isn't just a run of the mill gambler, losing but not more than he can afford to. He's got a serious problem." She pulled a sturdy, black tablet with no brand name on it from her bag and continued. "He's got six figures worth of debt. Upper six figures," she clarified just in case I wasn't getting the gravity of the situation, which I guess I didn't.

"I knew he gambled, but Ken never brought up money, definitely not that he needed it. He never asked me for any. Ever." It was probably the reason I'd stayed with him for so long, mistaking his foolishness for something deeper.

LOCKED

"Well, he should have, because he's in deep and," she held the word out for several seconds as her index finger swiped across the screen, "it looks like someone bought all but thirty-five grand of his debt."

She kept talking, using words that sounded like a foreign language to me as she explained the different ledgers she'd somehow managed to get photos of.

"I can't say for sure *who* bought the debt, but my money is on Farnsworth."

I groaned. "Not that name again. Who the hell is Farnsworth?"

Peaches shrugged. "It doesn't matter who he is because that changes regularly. What matters is *what* Farnsworth is. The answer is probably a ploy to get close to the ranch and take me out."

"Take you out? I'm guessing this is the mob version of taking someone out, not the rom-com version?"

Peaches nodded, and I shook my head, willing this all to be one big bad dream that had started the moment Ken came into my life. But all that did was give me a mild headache. And questions. "Why are you here? I mean you obviously have other choices, so why Opey?"

I heard, a little too late, how that question sounded and gave an apologetic shrug that Peaches waved off.

"I'll try not to be offended by that, Aspen." Her tone said she wasn't, and I was glad because I really wanted to know the answer. "I have a job, *had* a job. A good job that ended with some seriously fucked up people looking for me. And I'm still not completely sure if they're still looking. But Hardtail Ranch, Gunnar, and Maisie have been a safe haven for me. And then Gunnar stopped being a butthead and..."

Her words trailed off wistfully, sounding every bit like a woman in love. Then her gaze slid to her left hand and the big ass rock on the finger that told the world she was spoken for. It was gorgeous and clear and big.

"Wow. Congratulations, Peaches!" There was a genuine affection between her and Gunnar, but more than that they seemed to respect each other. I hoped they made it, but I wasn't convinced. "How do you feel about raising Maisie around a biker, uhm... motorcycle club?"

Her full lips pulled into a grin. "Sounds like you and Holden have already had that conversation." I rolled my eyes in response, not wanting to think about that again. Or *him*. Peaches continued, "If these guys are good enough to fight fucked up wars for the government, then they're good enough for me. Even better than that, they helped me when I needed it, and even when I made it impossible, they still helped. Let them do the same for you, Aspen. Whatever issues you and Holden have, he'll keep you safe."

"But that's the thing, Peaches. None of this trouble would've even come to your doorstep if I wasn't on the other side of that door."

She growled and then smiled before taking another sip of tea. "We don't know that, not yet. But regardless of your current relationship status with Ken, Farnsworth won't hesitate to use you against him."

I sighed and told her what I told Farnsworth right before he started manhandling me. "I don't mean a damn thing to Ken."

"Doesn't matter. It'll still be a message he'll get loud and clear. And next time, he might threaten someone *you* care about so you'll do or give him what he wants. Which we still have to figure out."

This was all too much. It was well above my comfort level and my ability to cope, and already I felt signs of a panic attack coming on. "I can't."

Peaches let her hand fall heavily to the table and sighed. "These guys, especially Farnsworth, are scary and what's going on is some scary shit, I know, believe me. But however tough and capable you *think* you are, the guys, the Reckless Bastards are that on crack. Army. Navy. Marines. SEALs. Rangers. Whatever gets your panties soaked, these guys are it. They've done and seen shit we can only imagine, and they lived to bitch about it."

"You should do publicity for the Reckless Bastards," I told her in an attempt to lighten the mood even though nothing about this conversation was light. "I get what you're saying Peaches, I really do, but I need to wrap my head around all this before I make any decisions."

Not that I had many choices. I could run on my own and let the chips fall where they may, or I could go back to Vance and put everyone I loved at risk. Neither of those was an ideal option.

Maisie ran back to the table, her little feet smacking hard on the linoleum, harsh breaths sawing out of her little chest.

"Aspen, I gotta message for you!" Her blue gaze bounced between me and Peaches several times until she caught her breath.

"Where did you get chocolate?"

"I won it," she said, sounding more like a teenager than a little kid. "Don't you wanna know about the message?"

"From who?" I asked because it seemed like the little girl might explode if she didn't get the news out.

She shrugged. "Some man said to give you this." She pulled a piece of folded up blue paper from the back pocket of her jeans and smacked it down on the table.

"He said to say, hang on." She squeezed her eyes tight as she tried really hard to remember the message. Her eyes popped open excitedly. "See you soon, Princess."

My stomach sank at those words because I knew exactly who'd been that close to Maisie. Talking to her. Close enough to hurt her. "Um, thank you, Maisie."

"Are you a real-life princess?"

I laughed at her exuberance over the possibility of a crown. "Nope. But I do have a couple of tiaras."

"Me, too," she said, flashing a wide, childlike grin before climbing into the booth and attacking her cold slice of pizza.

"What man, Maisie?" Peaches looked angry and terrified, but she was trying hard to shield Maisie from all of it. I didn't know how she did it, but I admired her ability to put the little girl first. Always.

"I don't know. Just some man. He was way tall and wore boots. Like Gunny, but he wasn't Gunny," Maisie replied and stuffed another bite into her mouth.

Peaches arched a brow in my direction, and the message was clear. *Told ya so.*

Yeah, she had. So had Holden. And now it looked like they were both right, and the danger was very real.

Apparently, this was my life now.

KB WINTERS

Chapter Nineteen

Holden

"These assholes, whoever they are, went too fucking far this time." Gunnar was steaming mad, literally, as he paced the length of the Sin Room, leaving the rest of us to watch him with our breaths held, hands poised to ward off the coming explosion.

"That fucker went after my little sister."

Not even an hour had passed since Peaches and Aspen had raced from the pizza shop after an almost certain encounter with Farnsworth, whoever the fuck he was.

"We don't know if it was the same Farnsworth who went after Aspen at her condo." Maisie's description hadn't been too detailed, only that he was really tall and had dark hair and big black boots. "We should assume it is until we know otherwise."

Wheeler stood and crossed his arms, staring at me as he spoke. "Are we absolutely sure the new girl didn't have anything to do with him showing up?" Even though the question pissed me off, I'd gone there immediately after hearing the story. "I mean, what are the odds he just happened to walk by while they were there having lunch?"

"Pretty fucking slim," Saint tossed out like a goddamn grenade. "But I'd say chances are better that he picked them up on the road to town and followed them. It's what I'd do." And just like that, the quiet kid had come to Aspen's defense with the most logical explanation.

Wheeler nodded and said, "I stand corrected."

"Peaches is already digging into the security footage of all the surrounding businesses to get a visual confirmation that it was the same asshole." Gunnar blew out a long breath that would've been accompanied by fire if it was at all possible. "We're pretty sure this somehow is about her."

It was a well-kept secret on the ranch that Peaches used to be some kind of super-secret hacker for the government until some job went tits up. She'd been running and hiding out on the ranch ever since, under the protection of the Reckless Bastards. "Why would they wait so long?" It just didn't make any damn sense. "And why Aspen's loser ex?"

"Maybe they *didn't* wait," Cruz added, his keen blue eyes missing nothing. "I mean we don't know that the fucker we killed in the bunkhouse wasn't a part of this. Or his shithead brothers."

Silence fell around the room as Cruz's words hit their mark. If he was right, we were too fucking far behind whoever was doing this and no closer to finding out why.

"Fuck!" The word was ripped from Gunnar's chest, a tortured sound that each of us could understand. "We need more information. Wheeler, I need you to reach out to whoever you can and see what else we can find about this Farnsworth fucker."

"On it. Plus we need to make sure one of us always has eyes on Aspen. Since you know her, Mah-Dick, I vote you do the heavy lifting on this."

"I *used* to know her," I clarified like it would make any damn difference. I'd already said I'd keep her safe, even if she was determined to be difficult about it. "It's taken care of," I grunted.

Cruz bumped my shoulder and let out a teasing laugh. "Aw, poor big dick Mah-Dick, has to keep a super-stacked blonde safe and secure on the ranch." For emphasis, Cruz held his hands out like big tits, squeezing them and pinching the nipples.

"Are you a fuckin' teenager, Cruz?"

He shrugged, not at all concerned about my attitude or tone. "Don't act like you haven't noticed how smoking hot she is, because no one fucking believes you."

How could I not notice, especially when she showed up every fucking day for work wearing jeans I swear she painted on just to torture me? "She's good lookin' all right. But that doesn't have a goddamn thing to do with keeping her safe."

LOCKED

Cruz snorted a laugh in response, and before I could wrap my hands around his scrawny pretty boy neck, a knock sounded on the door.

"What?" Gunner shouted.

There was no knob or handle on the other side of the door that led to the Sin Room, just a palm scanner Peaches had insisted on after all the shit that had gone down on Hardtail Ranch. Whoever was out there could only enter if they were allowed to do so. Wheeler yanked open the door ready to rip a new asshole to whoever it was.

"Baby Face, what the fuck do you want?"

Ford looked up into Wheeler's laughing eyes with a serious expression on his face. The kid was always serious, and no one had a damn clue why. He was good at his job, though, and proving to be a damn good prospect. "I, uhm...got some news."

Gunnar waved him inside, but to his credit, Ford stayed near the door and raked a hand through his curly blond hair.

"My buddy Fogel, we grew up and served together, he does some Uber-ing on the side and just dropped off Edna Mae's kin who came for a visit. Said he saw two guys wandering through the residential area and one of them had a tattoo on his neck that he tried to hide."

"Shit." Gunnar was up on his feet, and the rest of us followed seconds later. "Good work, Ford. Holden, let's go."

We moved fast, taking the ATV's back to where we all kept our bikes and headed into Opey. Fifteen minutes later we cruised into town, waving and smiling at the locals like it was a goddamn parade. It was more than the folks in Vance had ever given me and that only made me more determined than ever to protect the folks in this town. They were good, salt of the earth people, who didn't deserve this shit.

"There." I knocked on my helmet to get Gunner's attention and pointed to the middle of the block.

Two blocks over from where Ford's buddy had spotted them, which meant these assholes were either brave or stupid, casing a small town before the sun even set. Gunnar tapped his helmet and motioned for me to round the block and catch them on the other side. I did what he said and found the two in the same damn spot. Gunnar still watched from the end of the block as I swung my leg off the bike and approached.

"You boys lost?"

"Who the fuck is asking?" The shorter of the two was apparently the leader. At barely five and a half feet with two-toned hair and more ink than flesh, everything about this fucker screamed gangbanger.

"I am. You looking for someone or just looking to start some shit?" The other guy was taller but barely weighed a buck fifty. Judging by his demeanor, he wasn't the muscle.

"Hey, man, we don't want no trouble. Maybe we just want to look into some real estate."

"Nothing around here is for sale. I'll ask one more time, nicely." Maybe what I needed was to kick some ass. It would stop me from obsessing about Aspen, and daydreaming about sliding into her wet cunt again.

"We're lookin' for someone, man. No need to get your panties all twisted up."

"The only twisted up panties are the ones your mom left on my floor last night." It was childish as fuck, and I knew it, but it pissed him off enough to get in my face.

"Don't be talkin' about my mama, boy." The little one who was no bigger than Maisie stepped up to me. "I ain't afraid to kick a little cowboy ass. Ain't that right, Juno?"

Juno shrugged and kept his mouth shut, proving he at least had a few more brain cells than his buddy. "Let's just do this and get the fuck outta these sticks. I think I hear a fuckin' banjo playing in the distance."

Gunnar had gotten off his bike and slowly approached on foot, which meant I needed to keep these fuckers distracted for whatever he had planned.

LOCKED

"That's the music we play right before we toss some outsiders on the fire," I said and took a step closer. "Now tell me what the fuck you're doing in this neighborhood. If you came to harass anyone else, we can settle this right now."

Before he could say another fucking word, I had my hand around the little guy's throat, applying just enough pressure to make it hard to breathe. My gaze slipped to his friend who wanted to act but was too much of a pussy to do anything without backup. Or orders.

"Can't. Fucking. Breathe."

"That's kind of the point, asshole. Speak." He gave it his best shot, pawing and scratching at me to free him, but a few scratches were worth it because all that squirming gave me a good look at his neck tattoo.

"What the fuck are the Diablos?"

Gunnar crept up behind the scrawny guy without making a fucking noise, a feat for a man his size, and wrapped an arm around his neck, kicking the back of his knees to keep him off balance. "You look more like pieces of shit than devils to me," he said with a wide, almost pathological grin.

Now the little one really squirmed. "Let. Me. Go."

"Why are you here?"

"Fuck you, cowboy." He tried to spit, and I tightened my grip until his eyes started to bug out.

"Wrong answer, man." I looked past him to his friend. "What about you? Are you stupid like your friend? Or do you want to live long enough to fuck your woman again?"

It took him less than five seconds to make a decision. Maybe it was the implication he'd end up buried somewhere deep in the heart of Texas, or it could have been Gunnar's massive bicep cutting off his airway.

"Fuck it, Beto, I ain't going to jail for that crazy ass white boy." His pal Beto squirmed to break free, probably wanting to kick his friend's ass for folding like a cheap suit.

LOCKED

"Be more specific," Gunnar growled. "Which white boy? He got a name? A number?"

"Ken some shit or other. I don't fucking know. All I know is that white boy paid us thirty G's up front to come to this shit hole and fuck with some bikers. That was months ago, and he ain't paid us shit since."

The glare he sent Beto said this was a source of contention between them and that was some shit we could work with.

"Fuck with some bikers, how? Exactly."

"Just stupid shit. He hired some crazy ass motherfuckers, and they put an old lady in the hospital before skipping town, so he called the Diablos, that's us. Said to come down here and stir up some shit to draw out the bikers. That's it."

"What kind of shit?"

"Nothin' special. Trashed a B&B just to scare folks. That's all."

"And you only got paid once?"

"Yeah, but that fucker still wants us to do shit for him like we're some fuckin' domestic workers. Nah, homie. Fuck that boy."

Gunnar grinned behind him, but I wasn't happy. Yet. "Then what the fuck are you doing in this neighborhood?"

"Looking for that *puto* so we can get our money and get the fuck back to civilization." The way he snarled, all angry and squirming was understandable, but that didn't mean I believed these assholes.

"Take us there, and we're gone. At least I am," he said, glaring at Beto.

Gunnar let go of Juno, who fell to his knees and sucked in half a dozen lungfuls of breath before attempting to get to his feet. He looked at us, brown eyes wary but no longer afraid.

"I got some bad news for you boys and some worse news, which do you want first?"

"Fuck," Juno spat out. "We ain't getting paid."

LOCKED

"Nope." Gunnar made a popping noise and grinned, just to pour salt on the wound. "Ken is deep in debt, and it's all been bought up, so I'd say he's on borrowed time. And the B&B you trashed? Owned by some friends of ours."

Beto's face fell at that.

"And the worse news?" he said. Because a guy like Beto wouldn't be scared off by that kind of news.

"*We* are the bikers you were *half* paid to fuck with." The looks on their faces were fucking priceless. The smile Gunnar wore said he agreed.

Chapter Twenty

Aspen

"You gonna stand on my doorstep all night or you plannin' to knock?" Holden opened the door with a smirk on his face, arms crossed over his massive chest and drawing attention to thick, muscled biceps.

He looked so damned amused I didn't know if I wanted to smack that smile off his face or kiss it. Okay, I knew. I was totally leaning towards kissing that scruff. But that was not why I came.

"I hadn't decided who I thought would be better company, you or the door."

Holden's lips twitched, and I waited, leaning in anxiously to catch a glimpse of his real smile, the one he so rarely unleashed except when he was sweet-talking the horses. But once again, I was denied.

"Let me know when you decide." He stepped back and pushed the door closed. I stood there for a minute, sure he'd come back.

When he didn't, I dropped down in the cushion-covered rocking chair and took in the last rays of sun before the light disappeared and darkness took over.

"An apt metaphor, I'd say."

The sky grew darker and darker, the creepy vibe only lessened by the beauty of the stars popping out in the sky like diamonds.

I didn't care what anyone said, Texas was one of the most beautiful places on earth, and that included Paris and Tahiti. And Tokyo. Lightning bugs were already starting to fire the darkness that surrounded Holden's cabin. It was peaceful out here, peaceful enough that it was impossible not to think about the sharp turns my life had taken recently. Ken was shaping up to be my biggest mistake ever, one that very well might cost me my life.

"Made up your mind yet?"

Holden's deep voice startled me. I was so lost in my thoughts that I didn't hear the door open or his heavy footfalls on the porch.

LOCKED

"Don't sneak up on me like that!"

I was gifted with his deep rumbling laugh. "You're surprised to see me at my own house?"

"Not surprised, obviously, but I was lost in my own thoughts, and you startled me. How in the hell could a man so big move so quietly?"

"Training mostly. What's on your mind?" Instead of asking me to move or staring at me until I abandoned his extra comfortable rocking chair, Holden took the seat on the other side of the door, lowering himself with a grunt.

I shrugged and leaned back, blowing out a slow breath. "Nothing. Everything. The bunkhouse is too quiet." It was an oppressive kind of silence, the kind Daddy liked to bestow on those of us who dared *not* to live up to his expectations.

"In fact, it's damn creepy when you know there's a killer out there hunting you." Shit, I hadn't meant to say that aloud. Even though Holden said he wanted to help me, I didn't want to let him or anyone else know just how freaked out I was about all of this.

All of it.

"It's even quieter out here, but at least the company's good."

"It's getting better." And it was. Working with Holden wasn't as bad as I thought, and that was as much to do with the man as it was the horses and the tranquility of working the land. Hardtail Ranch wasn't as big as The Crooked H, my family's spread. There wasn't as much traffic and activity going around so I could get my chores done in comforting silence. It *felt* like a ranch should, not like a damn construction site.

"Thanks," he snorted and stood. "Come on inside, and let's have a beer."

"But it's so nice out."

"Let the mosquitoes feast on you, then." Without another word of concern for my skin, Holden stepped back inside the cabin and left the door open.

LOCKED

Stubborn man was just so sure I'd follow him, and I stood, casting one last glance out into the darkness, hoping there was no one out there watching, waiting for the right moment to strike, and then followed him inside.

"This place is great. I can understand why you chose it for the view alone."

"I didn't choose it." His voice sounded from the kitchen, and I was momentarily distracted by the sight of Holden's ass in denim, bent into the fridge so I could look my fill of those solid thighs cupped by well-worn denim. Damn, he was exactly what a man should be. He was big and hard and strong, and not at all concerned with being stylish or fashionable.

"Enjoying the view?"

His lips quirked in amusement but I wasn't ashamed to be caught ogling him.

"I am. Mind turning around for another second?" The laugh my words teased out of him made me feel twenty feet tall, like I had finally accomplished something in my life. Not something Daddy would be proud of, mind you, but an accomplishment all the same.

"Drink your beer, Aspen."

I accepted the icy brew and let the cool liquid slide down my throat until my body temperature dropped by a few degrees. Being around Holden confused me. It was arousing while somehow also being bad for my health. The man had a habit of making my heart race and my nipples harden, and he had the strangest habit of eliciting dirty thoughts whenever he was near. Sometimes even when he wasn't near.

"Who chose this land for you?" Was it a woman? Holden was too handsome, too kind to be single, but his gruff attitude could be a turn off for most women. I wondered if he had a sugar mama somewhere who'd bought him land to keep him close.

"I wonder what put that blush on your face," he said with an amused laugh.

LOCKED

I scowled and slapped both hands to my warm cheeks. "Probably the beer or the oppressive Texas heat."

"It was only eighty today," he said with a smugness that should have pissed me off, but it only turned me on even more. "Anyway the owner before Gunnar gifted it to me in return for helping him turn the ranch around. His kin had left the place damn near destroyed, and most of the animals had been abused and neglected. He gave me this plot."

"You are just one surprise after another, aren't you?" He shrugged one of those *aw shucks, ma'am* cowboy moves, and I laughed. "Why didn't you return to Vance and work one of the ranches there?" I held my breath in anticipation of a harsh rejection. It was clear that he didn't want to share the details of his life with me, and I couldn't blame him. But I also couldn't resist digging.

"Nothing for me to return too, not really. Ranch work gave me the solitude I needed to work through some shit. In Opey, I could do it without all the history."

Holden's tone said he didn't want to go into details about the shit he had to deal with, so I let it drop for now.

"Don't worry, Aspen, I didn't avoid Vance because of you." He didn't say it, but I was sure I heard the unspoken 'mostly' lingering in the air.

I didn't call him out, just nodded and tried to swallow down my next question. It was stupid to ask, but I had to. "But you left because of me?"

"In part." He looked me right in the eyes and told me the truth, which I appreciated. His nod was slow and thoughtful. "I was at odds anyway, no clue what I wanted to do with my life other than a life of back-breaking ranch work. You shuttin' me down the way you did, it left me hurt sure, and humiliated, but the next day I found my way to a recruitment center. Two hours later I was an enlisted man. Best and worst damn decision of my life."

LOCKED

"Why?" I knew he didn't want to talk about it and probably with no one less than me, but I had to know. The thought of what Holden had seen, of what that sweet boy I knew had witnessed and done in the name of his country made me uneasy.

"It just was." His gaze met mine, dark and angry and filled with some emotion I couldn't quite name.

"Did you lose friends?" It was a dumb question. Of course, he'd lost friends. Those damn wars were still going on. He probably lost more people he knew every day.

Instead of telling me to mind my own damn business, he kept it simple. "You could say that."

"But—"

"Drop it, Aspen." Ah, there it was.

"I'm just trying to get to know you, Holden. You want me to trust you with my life, to trust that you have my best interests in mind when it comes to Ken and to Farnsworth but that's mighty damn hard to do when—"

His lips cut off my stream of words. As far as ways to shut me up go, this one was my favorite, and the kiss, hot and hard and angry, was hot as hell.

I leaned into the kiss, into Holden's wide, hard chest and fisted the fabric in my hand because I couldn't seem to get close enough. His scent, masculine and earthy, sucked me in, and the way he controlled the kiss, hell the way he controlled me, was irresistible. His big hands fisted in my hair at first, tilting me back so he could devour my mouth with a ferocity I had never experienced. There was passion where you couldn't get enough of each other and then there was this, hot and primal and wild.

Holden tore his lips from mine, and a soft moan escaped as my body rejected how far away he now was. "You ask too many damn questions." His voice was gruff but not angry, his eyes were practically black with desire and his hands were strong and hot against my flesh.

"I'm a curious girl," I told him playfully, squealing when he lifted me onto the counter.

LOCKED

"Too damn curious," he growled, tearing the t-shirt I wore over my head and making quick work of the lacy bra too.

"Fuck, too damn gorgeous too."

His words produced a shiver that hardened my nipples, or maybe it was that dark gaze, so full of carnal promise that I didn't care that Holden did *want* to want me. Because he did want me and right now, that was all that mattered.

When his lips wrapped around one nipple and sucked it into his mouth, my head dropped back, and my eyes closed even as I arched into him, eager to give him as much of me as he could handle. "Yes, Holden."

The growl my words produced had a small smile curling my lips, and I let my fingers slide through his hair so I could hold him right where I wanted him. Where I needed him.

"More. Please." Holden released one breast with a pop and turned his attention to the other one while I let my hands roam every inch of him I could reach, starting with his strong, wide back. Reaching down for the hem of his shirt, I tugged it up and let my hands glide along the hard ridges of his back and then his chest before they found their way back to his thick hair.

"Fuck, yes, Holden."

He pulled back with another pop and a cocky smile that promised more.

"Such a dirty mouth." His hands were at my waist, unfastening my jeans and sliding them down my legs, taking my panties with them before I could take a second to reconsider.

"You like it." I could tell he did by the way heat flared in his eyes. "But I wonder if you like this more." My legs fell open and his gaze flew to my pussy, pink and swollen and dripping with desire.

"Fuck." The word came out on a primal growl that hit me right in the clit, and I moaned. "So fuckin' wet," he said.

One blunt-tipped finger rubbed the length of my swollen pussy, up and down those sensitized bits of

LOCKED

flesh before pushing the folds apart so he could get to the good stuff.

His fingers were a little rough, and that sharp contrast to the soft, slick skin of my clit was more than I could bear. My legs opened wantonly, begging for more.

"Holden, please."

"Please what, Aspen?" Before I could answer, one long thick finger slipped inside of me, and my pussy clamped down on it, pulsing and leaking like it was his cock.

"I can't hear you."

"Holden." The word came out harsh and guttural. My back arched into him again as his thumb slid over my clit.

"I need you. To. Fuck. Me." This time I didn't wait, couldn't. I slid to the edge of the island counter and pulled him by the waistband, making quick work of his belt, button, and zipper, using my feet to shove them down his legs.

"Now." I held his cock in my hand and moaned at how long and thick it was. *How could I have forgotten that?*

"Aspen." He grabbed my wrist, those blue eyes dark and close to the edge.

"Holden."

"You're playing with fire."

"No, I'm playing with your enormous cock. Is he ready to play, or do you need more priming?" My lips twitched at his offended growl, and I knew teasing him wasn't smart, but it was so damn fun.

"I'm always ready, sweetheart." As if to prove it, he laid one big hand across my chest and pushed me down, smiling at the squeal I released when the cool tile of the counter touched my hot flesh. "The question is, are you?"

I was more than ready, but before I could come up with something witty or flirty to say, he was sliding his ten impressive inches into my greedy little pussy.

LOCKED

"Fuck, I'm readier now." How the hell one man could be so gorgeous, so sexy and so goddamn blessed with that big cock, I had no idea, but I was happy that events had lined up as they did, and I got a chance to sample the delicacy that was Holden Jennings.

"More, Holden. I need more."

"What the lady wants," he said with a cocky grin that he'd already earned, but that determined look on his face was a sign of good things to come.

"The lady," he grabbed my hips and pulled me to him until my ass hung in the air and he was the only thing keeping me from falling. "Gets." The word was slow and torturous, nothing like the hard deep thrust of his cock deep into my pussy.

"Oh, fuck. Yeah!" He gripped me so tight I knew there would be bruises tomorrow, but I couldn't bring myself to give a damn, not when he was fucking me so good.

"Holden."

He was gone, pumping into me hard and fast and deep like he was on a mission, almost as if he was programmed to lose himself in my body.

"Aspen, fuck."

His hips moved even faster, and I felt goosebumps break out all over my skin, signaling my orgasm.

"Not yet," he growled and slowed his pace.

"What happened to what the lady wants?"

That fucker had the nerve to laugh when I was so close to that rush of pleasure that I could feel it in the air.

"The lady'll get what she wants when the man wants her to have it."

My response was to clench around his cock, letting my inner muscles pulse and squeeze around him until his knees went wonky.

"I hope he wants her to have it soon. Really soon."

"Fuckin' tease," he growled and snatched me off the counter. He walked a few feet until my back slammed against one of the logs that made up the four walls of the cabin.

"You want it?"

"Yeah, I do."

"You fuckin' want it, Aspen?"

Holy fuck, had anything so hot ever happened in my life? Nope.

"Hell, yeah, I want it. Give it to me, Holden. All of it."

He growled and slid all the way out of me, smiling at the sad choking sound I made before he slammed in hard. Deep. He did it again and again, leaving me no choice but to cling to him as he pounded his big, thick cock into me, pulling my orgasm closer and closer to the surface.

"Aspen," he growled, a warning that was unnecessary because I could feel the way his cock thickened and hardened inside of me.

"Holden, yes."

He growled again and swung me around, laying me across the kitchen table and grabbing my tits hard as he pounded into me with everything he had. His eyes were dark and unfocused, his muscles bunched and full of tension as his hips moved smoothly against mine. "Fuck!"

My orgasm started at my toes, making them curl next to Holden's ears while his thrusts came in shorter and harder that kept hitting the spot guaranteed to make me go cross-eyed. The moment the orgasm hit I felt full. No, *fuller*. His thumb slipped inside my ass, startling me at first, and then intensifying my orgasm until I couldn't think straight, couldn't see, couldn't do anything but feel the way his cock swelled inside of me as his hips surged over and over again.

"Holden, yes. Oh, fuck, yes!"

He growled and grunted and then froze before his body started to jerk with his own orgasm, sending another tidal wave through me that left me a sweaty, satisfied pile of woman. On his kitchen table.

"Damn."

I smiled. "I guess that's one way to get out of a conversation."

His deep laugh skittered over my sensitized skin and then his lips closed over mine hungrily, kissing me until I couldn't move.

"You complaining, sweetheart?"

"What are words?"

He laughed again, and I thought it was a sound I could easily become addicted to.

"Unimportant. Come on." He scooped me up off the table and tossed me over his shoulder like I weighed nothing, smacking my ass hard enough to send a flood of liquid between my thighs.

Holden carried me to his bedroom, and we spent the rest of the night avoiding conversation.

***

A low, anguished moan pulled me from a deep sleep, and it took me a few moments to realize where I was. Holden's cabin on the edge of Hardtail Ranch. After a long, exhausting night of the best orgasms of my life.

"No! Not Ria. It's not fuckin' Ria!" Holden's voice was loud and sharp, the pain so visceral it was like a vise around my heart.

"It's not Ria, goddammit!"

I sat up and looked at him through what I could see thanks to the moonlight spilling in through the curtains. He was asleep, deep asleep even though his face twisted in heartbreaking agony, the kind of pain I'd only ever read about.

I knew I had to do something. "Holden, wake up." I put my hand on his warm, hard arm and shook him gently.

"Holden, it's okay. You're just dreaming."

But his legs merely kicked harder, and he thrashed even more, getting his limbs tangled up in the

LOCKED

sheet draped across the middle of his body. I wondered who Ria was, this person who'd meant so much to Holden that he still dreamed about her.

What I wouldn't give to have touched someone that deeply *and* in such a positive way.

"Holden, wake up!" I shook him hard enough that the whole mattress moved, and his eyes snapped open. "Holden!"

Blue, almost black eyes opened, but whatever they saw, it wasn't me. And it wasn't now. I knew I needed to move, but his reflexes were quicker than mine. Before I could even take a breath, his hand snaked out and wrapped around my neck. Then, he squeezed.

Shit. "Holden, wake up! Wake up, Holden, it's me, Aspen!"

I smacked and scratched at his arm, even tried peeling his fingers off my skin, but none of it worked, dammit.

"Holden! Please, Holden. Stop." I stopped struggling, remembering that terrible advice from some self-defense class I took in college, but his grip tightened, and I couldn't get any air.

"Holden," I gasped.

He blinked, finally, and focused his eyes.

"Shit! Fuck! Goddammit!"

That was the Holden I knew, angry first, always. He swung his big, muscular legs over the edge of the bed and stood, stomping off to the bathroom and slamming the door behind him.

I gave him space to deal with whatever the fuck had just happened because I needed to deal with it too—and catch my breath. My gaze never left the door, even as I rubbed the skin on my throat. I'd be red and probably bruised in the morning, which meant I would spend the next seven to ten days wearing turtlenecks in the hot Texas summer. Where in the hell could I even *buy* turtlenecks in Texas?

Ten minutes or so passed before I found my courage and slid to the edge of the bed. I sucked in a deep breath that I let out for a slow count of ten. The few steps to the bathroom seemed to take forever, and all I could hear was my heart thundering in my chest. It even masked the sound of my fist on the door.

"Holden, open up."

He yanked the door open, an angry, emotionally shuttered look on his face that had me taking a step back.

"What do you want? You shouldn't be here, Aspen. Go home."

I laughed. "Home? I don't have a home, Holden, or have you forgotten?"

I shook my head and let out a bitter laugh. "You're gonna make me walk home in the middle of the night all because you had a bad dream?"

I snorted another un-amused laughed. "I guess I'm not the only asshole."

I stared at him for several long moments, hoping, waiting for him to change his mind. When it became clear he wouldn't, I shrugged, disappointed and turned to scan the room for my discarded clothes. *In the kitchen.*

"Shit. I'm sorry, Aspen, but you really shouldn't be here."

"Yeah, I got that part."

"Why the fuck do you want to be here, anyway? I almost killed you."

I whirled on him, my clothes suddenly forgotten in a mix of anger and sympathy and yeah, arousal at the sight of him naked.

"I care because I do, dammit. It's clear you're hurting, and maybe I can help."

He snorted, and I didn't miss the derision in that tone. "I'm beyond help, sweetheart."

"Oh, fuck you. Don't give me that *sweetheart* shit. You're hurting and crying out the name Ria in the middle of the night. Clearly, something is bothering you."

LOCKED

He opened his mouth, probably to say something shitty again and I pointed at him. "No! Don't even think about denying it. At least show me the respect of telling me to butt the fuck out!"

"Fine, butt the fuck out, Aspen! This isn't your concern. *I'm* not your concern."

He was right about that, but I was still concerned. Whatever demons gripped his mind, he was suffering, and I wanted to help.

"Fine, then keep your feelings to your damn self. Just lie down." One black brow arched in question, but he went to the bed and dropped down. Reluctantly.

"Happy?"

"Ecstatic," I deadpanned and pushed him onto his back. "Lie back, close your eyes and shut the hell up, okay?"

Holden, thankfully, nodded and kept that sensual pucker pulled into a straight line.

I climbed his body until I straddled his waist, feeling his half-hard cock pressed against my pussy, making me shiver. My hands went to his shoulders and started a deep, gentle rub until he actually relaxed. "Just breathe and don't think about anything."

He grunted a response but did what I said, which was all I could ask for, really. His body was still warm, almost overheated as my hands slid from his shoulders to his pecs, letting my fingertips and knuckles alternate to massage all the stress from his body.

"That's nice."

"Quiet," I said barely above a whisper because I didn't want to talk, either. Not about whatever he went through and not about Ria, whoever he or *she* was. His pecs turned to his abs under my fingers, and his breathing was slow and relaxed.

"Thank you for your service, Holden."

He grunted a response, and I smiled because it was exactly what I expected from him. Holden didn't join the Army for the accolades or the applause. He did it for a way out of his circumstances, and that only made his service even more noble.

LOCKED

I slid down his legs, digging my fingers into his hips and thighs, watching in stunned fascination as his big cock grew right before my eyes. It was magnificent, so long and thick with that imposing vein along the underside. Intimidating. I wanted it. My mouth watered for it, and I didn't know one red-blooded male who would turn down what I had in mind.

Kneeling between his thighs, I checked. Holden's eyes were closed. I knew they wouldn't be, not for long. With a smile I wrapped a hand around his thick erection and stroked, drawing a moan from him.

"Aspen," he groaned, and I just smiled.

"Fuck."

"Not now."

I didn't want to fuck him, not with all the emotions going through me right now, but I wanted to do something for him. For his pain. Lowering my head, I wrapped my lips around his thick cock and let my tongue slide up and down the underside.

"Oh, fuck!"

His hips bucked, sending that giant dick down my throat until I nearly choked.

"Sorry," he said.

"Don't be."

I was turned on as hell, but I didn't want to be, not now. I felt confused and angry, and maybe even a little hurt that after a long night of sex, he was calling out another woman's name.

Not the time; not the place.

I gave Holden's cock my full attention, licking and sucking it like it was my favorite flavor of a lollipop, and it kind of was. He was a little salty and tangy, hard and strong. I took him as deep as I could, keeping my eyes closed so that his sounds of pleasure guided me to take him over the edge.

"Oh shit, Aspen. Yes! Fuck, yes!" His body thrashed, and his hips bucked as his orgasm shot out of him with the force of a volcano, and I stayed there, right between his legs, sucking until his body was relaxed and his breathing had evened out.

LOCKED

Then I curled up beside his sleeping body, resting my head on his chest while I listened to him sleep.

For just a little while.

Chapter Twenty-One

Holden

Aspen was late for work and not just a few minutes late, no. An hour had already gone by. And her pretty little ass hadn't strolled over to the barn, or the stable, or the pastures, in jeans that were too damn tight for any man to focus on his work. Nope, she was a fucking no-show, and I was more pissed at myself for being surprised by her behavior.

No matter how hard she might have worked at The Crooked H, and I had my suspicions, she was still an over-privileged princess without any real work ethic. Hell, she probably thought because she spent the night in my bed that she didn't have to show up for work. That poor little Holden would do her work for her.

Well, she was wrong, goddammit, and to prove it, I let her chores go unfinished. If she wanted to earn her keep, she could do it the honest way. On her feet like the rest of us.

And yeah, maybe I felt a little bit guilty about what went down last night, or early this morning, which is why I hadn't yet stormed the bunkhouse to figure out what the fuck was going on. I owed her an apology for choking the shit out of her, for thinking she was someone else, an enemy in a distant land. For accepting the peace and comfort she offered without giving anything back in return.

"Dammit!" My head felt like a goddamn pinball, bouncing off thoughts of Aspen. The trouble with her ex, the trouble facing the MC, and as always, memories of the past. Of wars won and lost, of people won. And people lost.

It was too much. Too damn much, and this shit right here, the confusion and the turmoil was exactly why I didn't get too close. To anyone. Ever.

Still, Aspen had given me the gift of peace wrapped up in a good night of sleep. I owed her something. So when lunchtime had come and gone, I decided to go see what was up with the princess.

"Knock, knock, Aspen. Open up." I knocked first because I wasn't a complete asshole, and because this was her private space even if it was just temporary.

"Aspen, you're late for work."

She didn't answer and worry set in. Maybe she'd gotten turned around on her way back from my cabin and was lost in the thick brush or the waist-high grass where the semi-tamed land became wild.

"Shit." I pulled open the screen door that allowed the bunkhouse residents to enjoy some of the breeze that whipped through the ranch without letting in all the flies, gnats, and mosquitoes. The first thing I noticed when I stepped inside was the overwhelming stench of thick gas fumes, which didn't make sense because Aspen didn't cook. At least she hadn't since she'd come to the ranch, choosing to eat with Peaches and Maisie at the big house or grabbing one of the pre-made lunches Martha made for all the ranch hands.

"Aspen?"

Still no answer. As fear welled up in my gut, my feet carried me to her side of the bunk room. Neat and tidy as usual with no traces of her silky things or her expensive designer clothes. Just a leather duffel bag and a suitcase stacked neatly beside her bed. No photos or other personal touches. Everything about the space said temporary.

"Aspen!"

The lump under the comforter still hadn't stirred, which was just dis-fuckin'-respectful.

"Wake up!"

I threw open the curtains to let in a day's worth of sun all at once, and she still didn't move. My ego might like it if it had something to do with how good I fucked her last night, but something told me that wasn't it.

"Aspen, goddammit, wake up." Yanking the covers off her body, I grabbed her shoulder to shake her and found her skin cool to the touch.

LOCKED

And ashen. Shit, I couldn't wait for her to wake up because something was wrong. Seriously fucking wrong, and I had a feeling it was all my fault. I scooped her up in my arms, much as I had last night, except now she wasn't laughing or moaning with pleasure. Teasing me beyond all reason. This time she was chilled and damp, still out of it, and limp in my arms. My legs carried both of us across the gravel driveway to the big, gleaming whiteness of the big house.

"Stay with me, Aspen. Shit, stay with me. Please." The idea of losing someone else was too much. My whole body trembled with fear as I climbed the steps and stomped inside. "Gunnar! Peaches! A little help."

Dishes clattered in the kitchen when we arrived, and three sets of footsteps sounded before Gunnar and then Peaches appeared, followed by Martha Bennett, the cook and all-around mother hen.

"Aspen! What happened?" Peaches was at my side in a flash, putting a hand to Aspen's skin and smacking her cheeks trying to get her to wake up.

"No clue. She didn't show up for work, so I went to the bunkhouse and found her like this. The whole fucking place smells weird, like gas or something."

"Shit!" Gunnar was on the move, heavy boots thumping against the hardwood floor.

"Be careful, no sparks or sudden fuckin' moves, man!" He was already gone, and to her credit, Peaches' focus remained on Aspen, but I couldn't help but worry about Gunnar.

"Come on, let's get her upstairs, and I'll take care of her while you go make sure my man doesn't blow himself up."

"Deal," I grunted and followed her up the stairs. "You know what to do for gas poisoning?"

Peaches barked out a laugh at the top of the stairs and motioned for me to enter one of the guest rooms.

"I know what to do for alcohol poisoning or a drug overdose, a gunshot wound, but not gas poisoning. Luckily for Aspen, I know a damn good doctor. I'll give Annabelle a call while you get her settled."

LOCKED

Peaches left me alone, and I laid Aspen across the bed, cupping her face and willing her to wake up. I didn't even get the chance to do that with Ria, and I'd be damned if I lose another woman on my watch.

"Wake up. For once in your life, do what you're told, woman."

She coughed a little, but it was weak, the same as the flutter of her eyelids, but they finally revealed those beautiful blue orbs.

"Holden?" she muttered faintly.

"Thank fuck! How are you feeling?" She was weak and cold to the touch.

"Like. Crap."

The sound was so damn welcome I thought I might shed actual tears of relief.

"That's good. Any idea what happened to you?"

She shook her head and coughed again, attempted to sit up but a wince stopped her. "My head hurts like hell. What happened?"

Guess not. "Smells like a gas leak in the bunkhouse."

Her blue eyes went wide and then panic set in.

"Gas? You think someone did it on purpose?"

"No fucking clue, but Peaches is calling the doctor to come check you out, and I need...to go."

Why I felt nervous telling her that I didn't know, but I didn't want to leave her alone.

"I'm sorry, Aspen."

She frowned and tried to sit up again. "I don't need your apology."

"Too damn bad, you already got it." We stared at each other for a long, damn time, the air tense and silent between us. I didn't know what the hell she wanted but now wasn't the time. "I need to go check on Gunnar, make sure his dumb ass doesn't end up passed out in the bunkhouse. He's a lot heavier than you."

LOCKED

Her lips twitched, but she dropped her head back down onto the pile of pillows and let out a long sigh. "Go."

I got up from the bed, gave a sharp nod, and turned away, stopping at the door to give Aspen a last look, overcome with the sudden urge to kiss her. To make sure for myself that she was all right. I crossed to her bed, overcome at how helpless she looked.

"I'm so fuckin' sorry, Aspen." I pressed my lips to hers, a kiss that wasn't romantic or sweet or any of that gentle shit it should have been. This kiss was pure and simple, damn near obligatory, but it helped. She was safe. For now.

And I would make damn sure that she stayed safe from this moment forward. For now, I had to get Gunnar's back. "You still conscious in here, man?"

Gunnar appeared seconds later with a dark scowl on his face. "You're right. This shit was deliberate. Someone disconnected all the gas lines. What's the fucking smell in the air? Fuck!"

It looked like Ken and Farnsworth decided to bring the fight to us.

Well, bring it on motherfuckers.

Bring. It. On.

***

"You didn't really volunteer to go after this asshole just so you could show off your new truck again. Did you?"

I sat in the passenger's seat of Wheeler's brand new matte black SUV as we headed into Opey to see an asshole about a gas leak.

He laughed and smacked the black leather steering wheel with a whoop. "Not a lot of chances to drive on a ranch, at least not without getting this girl dirty."

He treated this truck like it was his baby, which was both comforting and disconcerting, but we all did what we needed to survive.

LOCKED

"What are you complaining about, anyway? You get to ride around in this bad boy, perfect for going incognito at night."

I snorted. "That explains the shade over the license plates. You're ridiculous, you know that, right?"

"Thanks, man. How's your girl?"

"She's not my girl," I said automatically. "And she's fine, or so she says. The doc says she needs to take it easy and no matter how much she complains, I'm making sure she does."

"Pretty short trip from hating her guts to willing to lay down your life for her." That was Wheeler saying a lot without a whole lot of words.

"It was more stung pride than hate." I was man enough to admit that now, given everything. "Besides, this has more to do with us than it does her." Ken had only come here at Farnsworth's insistence, for Peaches which meant for the Reckless Bastards.

"Whatever you say." Wheeler wasn't much of a sharer. He was a damn good leader and exactly the kind of man you wanted at your six when shit went down, but damn did he have the tense silence down to a science.

"Just be honest with yourself."

"I always am."

He pulled the car into a parking spot under a wide tree, and we got out to look at our surroundings.

"Always go in like it's a mission," he whispered more to himself than to me, but he wasn't wrong, so I put my game face on and squared my shoulders.

"The lights are on," I told him and pointed to Ken's unit. "I guess that means he's home."

"It might agitate your southern manners to show up without announcing yourself, but this is business." He flashed a smile and then squared his shoulders and hips before turning towards Ken's door.

"Asshole," I grumbled and followed him thinking about the last time I was here, saving Aspen from that handsy asshole. It seemed like a lifetime ago. How could it have only been a few weeks? It felt as if Aspen

LOCKED

and I had been in each other's lives for years. Decades, even. Not weeks.

As we drew closer to the door, Ken's voice came through loud and clear. "I said I was working on it, and I am. Don't you trust me?" That sleazy fucker lied as much as he breathed.

"You've been sayin' that for weeks, asshole. Time's up." Another man's voice sounded; one I didn't recognize.

Wheeler's gaze met mine, and he nodded toward the door, mouthing the words "Me first," as he pulled out his piece and turned the doorknob.

I pulled mine out and quietly followed him inside. Three men stood inside other than Ken; two were strapped and guarded the back room of the condo. The third had Ken's lapel fisted in his hand, his feet dangling a few inches from the ground.

"Did somebody have a party and forget our invites?" Wheeler flashed a crazy-assed smile, his piece aimed at one of the armed men while I aimed one at the other and their apparent leader.

"Bummer," the leader said, his smile fading. Quickly.

"Drop 'em. Now." The men heard the same steel in Wheeler's voice that I did, but they were either stubborn or loyal. Or just fucking stupid. Didn't matter which to me as long as they put their guns down.

"Or I can just put one in this dude's head. They both work for me."

I raised my gun even higher so it was aimed right at his head, just in case these idiots didn't get the message.

"Guns down," he growled and stood slowly, turning to size up Wheeler first, and then me. "And who in the fuck are you two?"

"I'll be asking the questions," Wheeler told the man, and I kept my gun trained on his goons. "Who are you?"

LOCKED

"Name's Giz, Sons of Wicked, Mesa Chapter. Enforcer. What business you Reckless Bastards got with limp dick, here?"

I blinked at the amount of information contained in that short sentence. Ken had somehow pissed off another MC. Dumb shit.

"You first," Wheeler insisted, and Giz shrugged like it was no big deal.

"This fucktard owes my MC thirty-five g's. He thought he could skip town and we'd just forget that he gambled more than he could afford to lose. Then he sent some wannabe assassin in black to try and buy the debt. We sent his ass packing, too, and now we're hoping Kenny boy here has had time to reconsider."

He smacked Ken's face hard but playfully.

Wheeler looked over at me. His expression mirrored my thoughts. *What the fuck did we just stumble into?*

I shrugged, and Wheeler turned back to Giz.

"You go after his ex to entice him to pay?"

Giz frowned. "Nah. She hasn't been around for at least the past week so we figured she grew a brain and dumped his sorry ass. Plus he's got a new piece, don'tcha Kenny boy?" His grip tightened, forcing Ken to choke out a breath.

"Save something for us," Wheeler told him, feet still rooted to the ground.

"Where's the fun in that?" Giz asked, eerie light green eyes wide and wild looking. He pulled his fist back with a laugh and unleashed it dead center on Ken's nose.

"You do something to your ex, Kenny boy? Are you one of those fuck tits who can't take rejection?"

When it didn't look like Ken would answer, Giz hit him again, this time the sound of crunching bone echoed in the living room.

"Answer me before I get mad."

"No," he finally said, but he was full of shit.

"I don't believe you," Giz sang and hit him again. "One more time." This time there was no pretense. Giz

LOCKED

pushed him against the wall and held them there with his forearm across Ken's throat. "You do something to your ex?"

"I didn't. I swear." The asshole couldn't even be bothered to lie well when it might save his life.

"I still smell bullshit." Giz hit him three more times, splitting open Ken's bottom lip and his left cheek.

"Okay! Okay! Fine, yeah I did something." He spat the words and sucked in oxygen. "That rich bitch thinks she can leave me for some fucking biker after all the time I put in? Nah, she's gotta pay since I didn't even get to her money. Yet." He let out a satisfied laugh. "Not so pretty with her skin all red and blistered, is she bubba?" His gaze slammed into mine, and I lost it.

My feet moved on their own, my boots loud against the hard floors until I was in his face.

"Her face is still as beautiful as fucking ever. How's yours?" Before he could answer, I punched him twice in the right eye. "If I catch you even thinking about Hardtail, I'll skin you alive and leave you for the fucking coyotes. Got it?"

He nodded quickly, eyes wide and terrified. "She ain't worth it, man. Trust me."

I punched him right in the fucking mouth. "You talk too much. That's for the biker comment."

Wheeler stayed where he was while I walked to the door and opened it. "We'll be right out front."

"I promise to leave him able to answer questions. From one MC to another."

Wheeler nodded and joined me outside. "That was some weird shit, right?" He shook his head like he couldn't believe what had just happened.

"Pretty fucking weird, yeah. But this is our life now, Wheeler."

"At least the enemies are clear out here." There was a weight to his words, and I knew he was talking about whatever it was he refused to talk about with anyone. Even his brother Mitch, the head shrinker.

LOCKED

"Yeah, but damn, is it me or does it seem to be more of 'em here in Opey?"

Wheeler's face spread into a wide grin that transformed him from an intimidating bastard into something else entirely.

"Nature of the beast, I guess. Especially with Peaches so connected to the underbelly of the government." Something he was all too familiar with since he did the blackest of black ops. "When this is over, hopefully, we'll be able to relax a little."

"I'll settle for a week, maybe two. Is that too much?" I didn't even want to think about what would happen with me and Aspen when this was all over, whatever the fuck *this* was. And I couldn't afford to think about it now, not with her safety on the line.

"You really think the gas line was Ken?"

"Fuck no. Probably can't even connect a stove without blowing himself up." Wheeler snorted and lit one of those black cigarettes he was fond of smoking.

They took fucking forever but damn they smelled incredible.

"It was Farnsworth, but he's just fucking with us."

"What makes you so sure?" Wheeler knew more than I did. He was all over this shit.

"Because he could have opened the valve enough to do serious brain damage or kill her altogether. This was just a warning. Ken took the credit because like Giz said, he's a limp dick."

Which meant this wasn't over, not yet. "What are the odds this Farnsworth will just give up?"

Wheeler shrugged. "Nil. We don't even know what the fuck he wants, only that he thinks Peaches has it or can get it for him."

"Fuck. A ranch shutdown is in our future, isn't it?"

Wheeler grinned just as the front door opened to reveal Giz and his backup.

LOCKED

"Damn straight it is." He clapped me on the back and went to have a word with Giz before we stepped inside to get a little info from Ken.

Chapter Twenty-Two

Aspen

Who would've thought a little invisible gas would have me laid up in bed for nearly a week? Certainly not me, but Dr. Annabelle insisted I take the nausea and dizziness seriously, which I did. Unfortunately, for the last five days, I woke up with a wicked headache and the kind of nausea that put my worst hangover to shame. But today I felt, not better, but not as sick, and my pain was minimum.

"Tell me the truth, Dr. Keyes."

Annabelle Keyes was what I would consider the perfect woman. She was beautiful with thick hair that she wore in a bun or a ponytail every time she stopped by to check on me. Her big brown eyes had bolts of gold lightning in them; her pale skin softened the harshness of her features. And to top it all off, she was a doctor. A beautiful female doctor. While I was just a woman with a trust fund. And terrible taste in men.

"Have you been taking it easy, Aspen?" She arched her brows, daring me to lie to her.

"I've been taking it comatose, Doc, I swear."

Between Holden and Peaches, I could barely get up to take a trip to the bathroom on my own. My meals were all served in bed, which was nice on days one and two, but by the third day I would've torn off my leg just to look at something other than the nice blue and white wallpaper.

Holden refused to let me do any kind of ranch work and thanks to the headaches, I couldn't do anything on the computer *or* watch TV.

"Tell me I'm on the mend. Please."

She laughed, and it was a feminine sound I wished I could pull off without sounding like I was offering up free blowjobs.

"How's the dizziness when you're up and walking around?"

LOCKED

"It happens so rarely, but today has been the best day so far. A little queasy, but if I start slow, it goes away. The head pain is about a three."

She nodded and looked up from her tablet. "Good. That means you're getting better, but it also means you have to listen to your body, Aspen. Don't push yourself out of pride or obligation. It will only take longer for you to heal."

"That wasn't what I wanted to hear, Doc." It was bad enough that I was technically sleeping with my boss, but not being able to work to earn my stay here, especially now, didn't sit too well with me. And I was honestly worried that I might offend Peaches if I just offered money.

"I know, and I'm sorry, but the good news is that you're healing. This isn't such a bad place to recover, is it?"

"No, but I don't want to be a burden," I told her around a yawn, feeling my eyelids start to grow heavy. "I'm tired of being a burden, Doc."

"Peaches isn't one to mince words. If she didn't want you here, she'd tell you. Rest up and find a way to pay her back. She loves shoes and gadgets. Now get some rest, and I'll see you in two days."

I nodded, but my eyes were closed before she reached the threshold of the room, and sleep claimed me. Sweet, restful sleep, thanks to whatever sedative the good doctor gave me.

When I woke up later, the sun was on the other side of the big house, and I slid my feet into a pair of gray bunny slippers and slowly made my way down to the first floor. It was late enough that the smells of dinner already hung thick in the air, and tonight smelled like it was gonna be some kind of stew and stew meant biscuits. That was fine by me.

This new version of Aspen was going to eat a biscuit whenever the hell she felt like it. No more snubbing my nose at carbs to please some man.

And it had absolutely nothing to do with the fact that Holden may have mentioned, once or twice, that he liked me with a little extra meat on my bones. Nothing at all.

"Move it. Not all of us can just lie around in bed all day." I turned at the familiar bitchy tone of Martha's twins. This one was bitchier by a mile, which made her Evelyn.

"I'm happy to shove your misshapen head into the oven and hold it there so you can have a few days off. If you'd like." I blinked innocently at her and moved past her with a well-placed shoulder check that jarred my head. Just a little.

"Bitch," she muttered.

"Yeah, don't you forget it." For good measure, I flipped her off just to let her know she couldn't push me around.

"Martha, what is that delicious stew you're making this time?"

She turned with a wide grin. "Thought I'd try something new tonight. It's a red wine beef stew with plenty of roasted garlic. Smells divine, doesn't it?"

"Pretty sure it's what got me down here in one piece."

At those words, Martha frowned and guided me to the kitchen table. "Have a seat, dear. I'll whip you up some cocoa since Dr. Keyes says you need to stay away from caffeine."

"Ugh, I forgot. Thanks, but I think I'll take it out on the back porch. Let the last of the sun heal me before it goes to bed on this side of the world."

"Sure. Just holler if you need anything."

"Thank you, Martha. You really are a gem." She reminded me of our cook at The Crooked H. Haley ran the household more than my mama or Daddy, and she made the best food in the world. Martha's cooking came in a close second.

She waved off my kind words and shuffled back to the stove, and I made my way outside. The sun rays streaked across the sky, warming my skin and tugging a smile across my face. It was nice to be up and walking around, even nicer to have no one hovering.

LOCKED

"I promise I'll do better next time, baby."

That voice belonged to Evelyn, I was pretty sure, and it came from the side of the house because that chick didn't do any work. Ever. "I know, but I had to move quickly. I thought I heard someone," she whined.

I shook my head because whatever it was, it sounded like Evelyn's boyfriend was asking her to do some sketchy shit. I had to catch myself from judging her too hard since I'd only recently extricated myself from the very same situation.

"I love you too, Kenny. You know I do."

It was a coincidence. Had to be. Ken was a common enough name for men of a certain age. Maybe I was at the stage in a breakup where I see his face and hear his name everywhere. Maybe. I didn't think so and leaned in for a closer listen.

She pouted and stomped her foot in the dirt. "I'll see what I can do, but I'm off for the next couple of days." The call ended after far too many kissy-face sounds, and when Martha brought out the hot cocoa, I was seated on the glider staring at the last bursts of sunlight.

I thought long and hard about the conversation I'd just heard. I was pretty sure it was Evelyn's voice but what were the odds she and Ken had crossed paths? I didn't know the answer to that either, but Opey was a small enough town, and they didn't live on the ranch.

Still, I would mention it to Holden next time I saw him.

Chapter Twenty-Three

Holden

It seemed like Farnsworth had gone back underground. No one had seen him, and not even Ken had heard from him in weeks. I wasn't dumb enough to think that was the last we'd hear of this Farnsworth or the next one, but I was relieved to have a reprieve from the constant tension. The quiet, though, it felt unsettling. Like it was too quiet. I didn't like it.

"Holden this is getting ridiculous." The minute my feet hit the floor of the porch the door swung open and my vision was filled with Aspen. Tall, blonde and angry. Very pissed off, in fact, but looking damn good in a pair of skintight jeans and a plain white tank she covered with one of those girly pink and green pearl snap button shirts. The perfect image of the sexy as hell farm girl. It was a far cry from the glamorous, showy girl she used to be and somehow, I liked it better.

A hell of a lot better. "Hello to you too, Aspen. I see you're feeling better." Once things cooled down and Aspen was well enough, I brought her to my cabin. I wanted her close. But, every time I looked at her, all I could see was her pale skin, thin pulse and discolored lips, remembered thinking she was dead, that I hadn't been able to save another woman. Seeing her all pissed off and fired up was better than out of it.

She growled at me and stepped forward, snatching one of the paper grocery sacks from my arms just so she could stomp off to the kitchen. Exactly where I was headed and she damn well knew it. "I've *been* feeling better Holden," she practically spit the words at me, whirling around the second my feet hit the tile floor. "You're the only one who doesn't seem to notice." She grabbed a beer from the fridge and turned to me, daring me to tell her she shouldn't be drinking yet. It was too soon. "I can't just sit inside your cabin all day. Every day."

I understood all that, I really did. But I had priorities too. "I want to keep you safe, Aspen. If I had checked on you earlier instead of," I paused because it didn't really matter why I didn't check on her, only that I hadn't. "If I had checked on you earlier maybe you would be recovered by now, I don't know. But I'm sorry and I'll do better." It was a promise I planned to keep.

Aspen sighed and rolled her eyes, giving all her attention to the beer before her gaze swung back to mine. "It's over, Holden. It happened, and I'm fine. Besides, if you're gonna leave me alone all day I'd rather it be at the bunkhouse where I might encounter a person now and again. Out here I'm just...alone."

"Bunkhouse? Are you crazy?"

She was hamming it up to make her point, but dammit she wasn't wrong. My cabin was too remote to get to her fast if she needed me, another damn oversight on my part. "Fine." I grumbled. You can come with me until this shit is settled."

A disgruntled snort came out of her, shocking the hell out of me. It was the only thing truly shocking about her response. Aspen was shit at hiding her emotions.

"So what, now I'll just be your shadow? Your assistant?" Arms folded, and her blue eyes breathing fire, she was breathtaking in her anger. "I don't think so buster." And frustrating as hell.

"Buster?" I was learning to read her well. Aspen didn't like to be guided. She needed to make decisions on her own.

"Not my shadow, although, I have to say that I do like the sound of that. But no, that's not what I had in mind." Although, now that I had the thought, my mind refused to let it go.

"Explain."

"You do what I do, when and only when you can handle it."

"I can handle it," she insisted quickly, notching her chin up in defiance.

"If you say so you can prove it to me. Starting tomorrow." I let out a long breath.

LOCKED

"What's up? You're worried about something," she said, her voice softer and filled with concern as she tore the brick of cheddar from my fingers. "Talk."

"It's too fucking quiet," I admitted to her after a long, thoughtful silence. Aspen wouldn't want me to sugarcoat things for her, and maybe if I was straight with her, she'd take my words seriously.

Her laugh was low and throaty and feminine. "Isn't quiet a good thing when it comes to this type of stuff?"

"It is, but this feels wrong. It feels unsettled like maybe it's the calm before the storm. I always hated that fucking expression, you know that? It's not calm before the storm. It's a swirl of energy that's impossible to ignore only it's so strong that you know you can't fight it. It may seem calm, but it's not."

"You really think so?"

I looked up into sincere, sober blue eyes and saw that she was asking for the honest to God truth. "I do."

"Okay, then. I'll continue to be careful while I stick to you like flies on honey."

"Maybe not that close. I still have a ranch to run."

She laughed again, and the sound was soothing. "But I need you to be diligent and careful. If you see or hear something that seems off, even if you don't know why tell me."

She nodded. "I will. I promise." To punctuate her words, Aspen laid a hand on my chest, and she kept it there until she tamed my heart, slowing the thumping rhythm with her nearness. "I swear it, Holden."

"Good." I didn't want her to see how relieved I was that she would finally start cooperating with my desire to keep her safe.

"Hungry?" I asked and turned to put the groceries away.

"In a way yes," she said, voice pitched low and sexy, drawing my attention.

LOCKED

I looked back and found Aspen standing just a few feet away from me, the pearl snap shirt sitting on the counter, her hands tugging on the hem of her tank top, a determined look set in her big blue eyes. Pink nipples hard and mouthwatering, her slender waist begging to be held in the confines of my grasp. I couldn't resist her, but I had to be certain.

"Are you sure, Aspen?"

KB WINTERS

Chapter Twenty-Four

Aspen

I stood there naked from the waist up in the middle of his rustic country home-style kitchen, his gaze glued to my tits, and he was interrogating me?

"What do you mean, *am I sure?*" This man was bound and determined to drive me out of my damn mind.

"I would think this is all the proof you need, but maybe you've taken a few too many shots to the head."

It probably wasn't smart to rile him up, but it was better than having him look at me like some damn wounded bird.

"Aspen," he began but stopped to bite out a curse when I slid my jeans over my hips and down my legs, giving a little shimmy as I stepped out of them.

"Yes, Holden?" My gaze never left his as I slid a pair of plain black silk panties down my legs and kicked them his way. "What is it now? Do I not know my own mind anymore?"

"I didn't say that," he stammered, but the heat in his eyes went a long way to making me a little less pissed at him.

"So is it that you think you know more than Dr. Keyes?"

"Of course not, I just want you to take it easy."

"And I am, but if I don't get moving, then I'll never feel a hundred percent. And sex, in my professional opinion, is the perfect way to ease into the rigors of ranch work again." It was a stretch, but I was desperate. For him and for something other than the four walls of this cabin.

"But Aspen," he began and stopped, raking a hand through his thick dark hair, blowing out a frustrated breath. I felt bad for Holden, denying what he wanted so bad in an effort to be a gentleman when he didn't need to try so hard. He was truly one of the good ones.

"No buts, Holden. Unless of course, we're talking about this one." I turned with a sultry smile at him over my shoulder and gave my ass a smack, hoping to entice him to give me what I wanted. What we both wanted.

"Dammit, woman."

Yeah, that tortured sound right there, it was one I was starting to grow attached to. Just the sound. Not the man.

"You don't want this, Holden? Because I've been dreaming about getting you naked again and running my hands all over your big naked body. Tasting you again. Having you lick me until I explode."

He sucked in a breath, and I stepped closer. "You'll tell me if it's too much."

"I'll tell you if it's too much," I repeated back to him absently, my mind focused on stripping him out of those tight cowboy jeans that had a starring role in my shower fantasies. "I promise."

"I'm holding you to that," he said and grabbed me by the waist, hoisting me up on the counter and pushing me down. "Hold your feet right here," he said as his big hands covered my toes that hung over the edge of the counter as he spread my legs. "Yeah, don't move."

"Not sure I could if I wanted...to!" Holden dove right in once he had the green light, burying his face so deep in my pussy that my hips bucked up over and over again, eager to get closer to him. It was magnificent the way he used his tongue to ratchet up my desire, to slowly drive me insane as he slid a finger in and out of me, coating it with my juices.

"You're so fucking wet, Aspen."

"I'm so turned on I could burst, Holden, I swear!" Maybe at another time in my life, another place I might have been ashamed of the way I rubbed against him like a cat in heat, but not today. Not in this moment and definitely not with this man. The more I moaned and purred and begged for more, the more he gave me. It was always more intense than before, harder and rougher too. It was perfect. "Holden, please!"

LOCKED

"Please, what darlin'? You want more of this?" He held my legs apart and blew until my clit swelled and pulsed with nerves, then his tongue curled around the sensitive knot, and I bucked up against him so hard my vision blurred.

"Or maybe this." His tongue flicked over my clit at lightning speed, feeling as good as my vibrator.

"Yeah, that. Fuck yes, that!" I grabbed a handful of his hair and ground my hips against him, drawing another growl from him that sent shivers through my body. "Even better," I purred as he worked swiftly, efficiently to bring me to the edge just so he could slow time down while I drifted over the side.

Then my body was floating high up in the sky with giant, bursting fireworks going off in the background while I slowly made my way back to earth with a smile on my face.

"Even better than what?"

When I came back to earth, my sleepy satisfied gaze crashed into Holden's amused blue gaze. "What?"

"Right before you came you said 'even better,' and I want to know, even better than what?"

Shit, had I said that out loud? Judging by the smug smirk on his face, I'd say yes. "That tongue of yours is even better than my favorite vibrator."

His laughter came low and deep as he positioned himself between my thighs, stroking his cock and sliding it along the length of my pussy, drawing sharp gasps of air from me. "Thanks."

"I should be. Thanking you," I told him, gasping and arching into the thumb he slid into my pussy. "I might still be thanking you."

He laughed again and slid his cockhead into my body, giving me time to adjust to his enormous cock.

"Believe me, Aspen, the pleasure was all mine."

"So far I'd say it was mostly mine." My thighs still quivered in proof of the pleasure he'd given me. But then his thick cock was sliding in and out of me, and it was hard to think about anything except the way he seemed to touch all my nerve endings, every pleasure zone in my body lit up whether he was sliding out or thrusting deep inside. "Oh, fuck!"

"Agree. To. Disagree." He punctuated every word with a swirl of his hips, a hard deep thrust that sent lights flashing behind my eyes. I didn't know how I was able to take his big cock, but I knew that I felt like I might die without it, without the skillful way he pumped hard and gave me *almost* too much before pulling back and sliding in slow and gentle.

It was an intoxicating blend of rough and tender, intense and easy, too much yet not enough. My body was on overload. "Holden. Please." I lifted my legs and my hips, wincing at the pain of adding more of Holden but desperate to have as much of him as possible. "Please."

Suddenly I was airborne with two strong hands gripping my ass, my back pressed up against the sturdy door that led to the backyard, my body sliding down his thick cock with the help of my arousal and gravity. "You want more?"

"Yes. Please." I nipped his ear and scraped my teeth along his neck. That seemed to have snapped some button inside of him. His fingertips dug a little deeper into my skin, and he thrust a little harder, a lot deeper with a much hungrier growl.

"Fuck, Aspen. I can't hold back."

"Don't. I want you, Holden. All of you."

"Aspen!" He gripped me hard as he turned away from the door and laid me on the kitchen table, letting one hand slide up the center of my body to my throat while he pounded into me, hard and fast, and with an intensity that would have been frightening if my body wasn't a mass of nerves and sensations.

"Holden, I'm there." At my words, his hands gripped me tight enough to sting, and he pounded so hard, and so fast I knew I'd be bruised tomorrow, but I couldn't bring myself to give a damn, not when pleasure flooded my body and sent shockwaves through my veins.

"Oh, Aspen! Oh, fuck!" His hips moved lightning quick, and then I felt his cock thicken before a surge of liquid pulsed from his body to mine, hot and slow, connecting us down to our souls. My orgasm flowed through my body, and one twitch of his hips could send another one starting again.

"So good," I panted. "So, so good."

Holden laughed and kissed me slowly like I mattered to him.

He kissed me like I'd always wanted to be kissed but had given up hope of ever having, because, well, because men sucked.

"I'd come up with something better, but I'm pretty sure you've fried my brain."

Mine too. That was the only excuse for what came out of my mouth next. "Mine too, but I think you just loosened a memory from my goofy head."

He froze and looked at me, his gaze serious even as his chest still heaved from our lovemaking. "What kind of memory?"

I shook my head, trying to remember the details. "I heard one of Martha's daughters on the phone with a man she called Kenny. I don't remember everything now, only that it sounded suspicious, and I wanted to remember so I could tell you."

It sounded flimsy even to my own ears, but the dark look on his face ruined my post-sex haze.

Chapter Twenty-Five

Holden

"Why did you wait so long?" It wasn't a deliberate act, at least I didn't want to believe it was, but the thought came instinctively. "Well?"

She sighed in front of me with a mouthwatering set of tits that made it hard to have a serious conversation. It was damn hard, but I managed to meet her gaze.

"I forgot, okay? It was the first day I didn't feel completely awful, and I overdid it with Martha's stew and the cake. And the ice cream. I barely made it to bed before I shut my eyes."

She hadn't *even* made it to bed that night, dozing off at the kitchen table with her head resting on my shoulder. I lifted her in my arms, reveling in the feel of her warm curves pressed against my body, and carried her to bed myself.

"And no other reason?"

Something like hurt, or maybe it was guilt, flashed in those light blue eyes that were now dark and stormy. I saw the moment my words sank in because she blinked all emotions but anger.

"Right. *Of course.* You think I *conveniently* forgot to what, to help out Ken somehow?"

She shook her head and scooted down off of the table. Her gaze scanned the room until she found what she was looking for. Her panties.

"Unbelievable. Really, you are un-fucking-believable, Holden." She yanked her bra off the floor and put it on, disgust dripping off her every move.

"Just when I think things have changed or were *maybe* starting to change, you remind me why it never will. Well, thanks, Holden."

She shimmied into her jeans and tank top, tucking the other shirt into her back pocket.

"What else should I think, Aspen?"

She sighed. "Apparently, you'll always think the worst, no matter how much time and distance have been put between me and that arrogant high school girl I used to be. So keep on thinking that."

"Try telling the truth."

"I never lied to you. Not once. What reason would I have when your opinion of me couldn't possibly get any lower?" She shook her head, blonde hair still mussed and along with those kiss-swollen lips, even angry she looked gorgeous as hell.

"Another lesson learned, I suppose."

Without another glance or another word, not even an argument to reconsider, she walked away.

She needed a few minutes to cool down, and then we could have a reasonable conversation. At least that was my thinking before I heard the front door open and close and realized the stubborn damn woman had left. The sun had set long ago, and even with a flashlight, the walk back would take about thirty minutes.

Alone.

"Shit!" I stepped into my jeans and boots, grabbing a t-shirt on my way out the front door.

"Aspen, get back here!" I darted back inside the cabin to get my flashlight and scanned the area beside the house for a beam of light.

"Aspen!"

"Go back inside, Holden."

I followed the sound of her voice. "Dammit, woman, stop running from me. Get back here, and we'll talk. Like adults."

"Because insulting me is gonna get you your way? Go screw yourself, Holden."

I could hear the heaviness in her breathing, but the grass was so goddamn thick and so tall, it was hard to see much of anything beyond the occasional splash of light.

"Look, Aspen, seriously. This isn't funny."

"Who's laughing, Holden? You just fucked me and then insulted me before the jizz was dry. God, just go away. Please!"

"Can't do that, sweetheart." When she put it that way, I had sounded like an asshole, but somebody had to ask the questions. It was better to be up front than to spare feelings, right?

"I'll see you to the bunkhouse, and then I'll leave you alone. Okay?"

"No. I don't need you to be my babysitter. Oh!"

A whizzing sound and then another followed the sound of two gunshots.

"Shit! Someone's shooting!"

"Down, Aspen, get down!" I couldn't hear what direction the shots were coming from. Yet. "Turn off your flashlight."

"How am I supposed to see?" Her words came out on a sharp whisper, which would make it hard for the shooter to see us without high-grade military equipment.

"Just keep telling me what an asshole I am, and I'll follow the sound of your voice."

"Glad you can crack jokes at a time like this." Her displeasure was easy to hear, but still, I smiled. Another shot rang out, and Aspen shouted, giving the shooter a clear line to our location.

"Quiet, Aspen!"

She breathed loud enough that I could hear her, but she was low to the ground. When I found her, that pretty face was about two inches from the ground.

"Over here," she whispered. Angrily.

"Hey, did you miss me?" I knew I was close, but I couldn't risk turning my flashlight on.

"Shut up." She smacked my chest, and that was how I found her.

"You did miss me." Another round of shots rang out, and I dropped down, draping my body over Aspen's. "Can't say this isn't what I was hoping to be doing right about now."

"Too bad about your big damn mouth and your suspicious mind. Oh, and let's not forget your cynical heart."

LOCKED

I grunted. "Maybe we can have this discussion when bullets aren't flying all around us?"

"Then maybe stop pressing your fat fucking cock against me." She sounded annoyed, but that little hitch in her voice said she was also turned on. At a moment like this. "Where do we go?"

"West. There's a supply shed about eight hundred feet west of here."

"West would be?"

"Go to your left, Aspen. Stay close." I turned on my flashlight and tossed it to the right. "Run and stay low!"

We took off together, running low while the sound of the shots grew more distant. The grass was tall, and the mosquitoes were all over the damn place, but we made it to the shed without any bullet holes piercing our skin.

"Shit, shit, shit!"

I stepped up behind Aspen and put a hand over her mouth. "Shhh, we're not in the clear yet." I kept one hand wrapped around her and the other turned the shed's knob and pushed. "Step up once and to your left."

As soon as we were inside, she smacked my shoulder. Again. "Don't sneak up on me like that!"

"I was behind you the entire time, Aspen. I know it's scary, but please, try to stay calm." I put my hands on her shoulder to steady her. "It's cramped in here, and we can't use the flashlight to see our way around. That's probably for the best, so we don't make too much noise.

"What is this place anyway?"

"You mean in all your ranch work you never ran across a storage shed? There's an old tractor in here, some shovels, and pitchforks, an old pickup truck. Some other junk."

She glared at me. "No. Daddy had buildings built for that kind of thing. Likes to keep the ranch looking streamlined."

LOCKED

Good, keeping her annoyed and distracted kept her from freaking out, and that was my number one priority. Number two was getting some fucking help.

"See what happens when you venture outside without me?" My timing was bad, but our proximity was good, plus I just couldn't help myself.

Neither could Aspen, apparently, because she stepped in close, looked me right in the eyes, and punched me in my arm.

Again.

KB WINTERS

Chapter Twenty-Six

Aspen

Holy. Shit. Someone just shot at me. A lot. Or maybe they were shooting at Holden? He *is* in a biker gang, which pretty much guaranteed somebody was always shooting at him, doesn't it? Not that I could talk, though. My ex-boyfriend had somehow gotten hooked up with a black ops dude with a penchant for causing pain. The more I thought about it, the more those shots could have been meant for both of us. Crap.

"Any idea who that was?"

"How in the hell should I know? I've been chasing you through the damn fields for the past half hour, maybe longer."

Even in the dark, I could hear the scowl that marred his handsome face when something pissed him off.

"Don't yell at me, damn you, Holden. I didn't ask you to follow me, did I?" It was a childish response; one

Daddy would have bitched about until I apologized or rephrased.

"Yeah, well, I didn't ask you to run out of the cabin like your ass was on fire, did I? Nope you did that all on your own, which meant I had to run after you, without my gun, into a gunfight."

Okay, yeah, so maybe he had a point. Still. "Sure, Holden, this is my fault. You fucked me and then insulted me, but somehow this is all my fault. Sure."

Sometimes I wondered why I even bothered with men, but the twinge in my thighs and the way my pussy pulsed, even now moments after escaping death, was a keen reminder.

"I never said that."

"You didn't have to, and I'm done talking about it." I thought it might be best if I was done talking to Holden for a good long while.

"Fine. Did you grab your phone before you stormed out of the cabin?"

LOCKED

"Of course, I did, since I didn't think I was coming back. I already activated the green button on that app Peaches installed on my phone. She said it was perfect for when the shit hit the fan. I think this qualifies."

I could only see his outline in the tiny sliver of moonlight that crept through the wooden slats at the top of the shed. "Good. That means they should be here any minute, hopefully, armed."

Good. That was exactly what I needed, a reprieve from Holden's proximity. Being around him made it hard to think, hard to focus on anything but his big body and masculine scent. "Can't wait."

"That eager to be rid of me? Didn't take you long to grow bored, I see."

I refused to let him taunt me. I may have a shitty record when it comes to men, and maybe even being a good person, but I wouldn't rise to the bait. I wasn't wrong this time, he was, and I refused to take the blame for someone else's mistake.

"Nothing to say?" he said in that gotcha tone. "That has to be a first."

Oh he was so damn smug, wasn't he? "There's a first time for everything." That was all I felt the need to say, drawing into myself until I heard engines in the distance.

"You'll have to talk to me sometime, Aspen."

That's where he was wrong. "What would you want to talk to me about, Holden? I'm just a ditzy blonde trust fund slut, oh and a backstabber. Seems like you got away just in time." With that parting shot, I patted his chest and walked past him and out of the shed to greet the Reckless Bastards.

My unintended heroes.

"You doin' all right, sweetheart?" Slayer was the first off his four-wheeler. He strolled up to me with all the swagger of a movie star and wrapped an arm around me.

"Better now. Thanks for coming to get me." My gaze found Gunnar and his permanent scowl, and I nodded my thanks because I knew that was all a guy like him would accept.

"Did you see anything?" Gunnar asked.

"Not even a muzzle, but I think the shots came from behind us. I never saw a flash of light, but then I wasn't looking for it, either."

"Okay. We'll get you back to the cabin—"

"That won't be necessary. I was headed back to the bunkhouse when this happened. I'll just go over there since it's on the way."

Whatever he wanted to say, Gunnar kept his questions to himself, and I was grateful for it. "All right."

I stood off to the side and out of the way, watching the bikers interact. You could tell by the way they walked, the way they carried themselves that they were all former military. The currently tense set of their shoulders said they were all on alert.

Gunnar was the clear leader. The man had the weight of the world on his shoulders, and Wheeler was his clear number two. But right now, they worked like a solid military unit, scanning the area for tire tracks, cigarette butts, anything that might indicate who was out there.

"We're clear. Let's head out but keep your heads on a swivel!"

"Hop on," Slayer said with a knowing smile. "Still doing all right?"

"Considering I've never been shot at before, I guess this is as okay as I'm supposed to feel," I said.

"Well you know what they say, you always remember your first time." Slayer flipped his hair over his shoulder and slid in front of me. "Hang on tight. I like to go fast."

I held on to Slayer's hard body and closed my eyes, letting the cool night air wash over my skin as we made our way back to the big house. And I didn't look back at Holden once.

Progress, as they say, comes in small steps.

Chapter Twenty-Seven

Holden

"I am fucking, so fucking tired of always *re*acting. We need to be proactive from now on."

Gunnar had a point, and we all felt his anger as we stood in a circle, cramped in his office in the main house because he refused to leave the women unguarded. "Do we know anything yet?"

"Not enough. But I suspect whoever did it didn't just get lucky. They were waiting. Hell, they would've been waiting until morning if we hadn't been fighting."

Still were fighting if the way Aspen had given me the cold shoulder was any indication. She hopped on the four-wheeler with Slayer and let him whisk her away without one look back at me, the man who was between her and the bullets.

Cruz laughed and shook his head. "Still your same old charming self, eh?" They all had a good laugh until Wheeler spoke.

"It's probably a good thing. I would've waited until you were asleep and put two in both your heads." That sucked all the laughter and oxygen right out of the room.

"Way to make it dark and fucked up, Wheeler." Cruz snickered again, and even though Slayer elbowed him in the side, I admired the man's ability to laugh even when shit started to look bleak.

"What? That's the truth. That fight probably saved both your lives." Wheeler meant it, which was fucked up in its own right, but also what got him out of the service in one piece. Physically, anyway.

I snorted out a laugh at his logic. "Try tellin' Aspen that, would you?"

"Sure." More laughter went up, which might seem odd to anyone listening, but this was what we did. Laughed through the tough shit because that was how the tough shit got done. Humor and levity helped you stared death in the face and do the impossible time and time again.

LOCKED

"Wheeler's right. Now we have the chance to act first." Gunnar had a determined look on his face, and I took a couple of deep breaths, taking my time to exhale because I knew this meant game faces on.

"No offense, Prez," Saint began in his quiet, certain style, "but we don't even know who did this yet to form any kind of plan."

"I know that," Gunnar snapped, more upset at the situation than the messenger. "That means we need multiple plans. One for Ken and one for Farnsworth."

Before Saint could ask another question, I had one of my own. "You think there's a possibility Ken *isn't* acting on orders from this Farnsworth character? Maybe he's a dick all by his lonesome?"

"Could be, but if it was Ken waiting out by your cabin, that means he's after Aspen. From everything Peaches has said, his crazy is more of an act."

"So we don't have to worry about him coming after Aspen? Or we do?" Cruz asked the most damn questions, but Gunnar didn't seem to mind.

"Make no mistake, he'll kill her if he needs to, but it's unlikely." Before Gunnar could say anymore, a knock sounded. In the split-second Saint and Slayer went for their weapons, Wheeler's was already aimed dead center at the door.

"Come in."

Blond curls appeared first, and then the ridiculously boyish face of our first prospect, Ford, appeared.

"Is it a good time, sir?" He wasn't allowed to attend any meetings in the Sin Room, and being so fresh from the service, the kid still had a healthy respect for hierarchy and formality.

Gunnar waved him in. "I told you to quit it with the sir, shit. This ain't the service. This is a brotherhood."

"Right," Ford said, face fixed into a blank expression before he jumped into his business. "Ken wasn't at home. The place is dark and locked up like he left voluntarily. His car wasn't in the designated spot or the garage, or the office he rented to keep up his businessman image."

Ford paused and looked up to Gunnar for the okay to continue, which he got.

"Nobody's seen his car in town for the past twenty-four hours, and I did a block by block drive through the town. Nothing."

"Good job, kid. Grab some food from Martha and keep watch out back." Ford nodded at Gunnar and left without another word.

"Goddammit, this motherfucker—whoever he is—came on to our property and shot at one of us. This shit won't stand. It can't."

"I agree," Wheeler added. "We need to do another sweep of the property and we need more weapons." His brain never shut off. I was pretty sure Wheeler dreamed of ops and logistics, probably why he was more fucked up than the rest of us.

Gunnar nodded, grateful for that twisted mind, I was sure. "Saint, grab Ford and go load up the truck from the armory. And watch your fucking backs. Please."

That one growled word said how worried he was, and I didn't blame him one fucking bit. Chances were good that his woman was the target of all this. My woman, too, if that was what Aspen was to me, or wanted to be anymore—anyway, she was just collateral damage. A means to an end.

Saint nodded and stood. "Any requests?"

"Grab me another knife, one for my new ankle sheath," Gunnar said with a wild-eyed smile. and unstrapped it from his leg, handing it to Saint. "Thanks, bro."

Saint flashed another look around the room, and when no one spoke, he left. The room fell into a tense silence, and I wondered where Aspen was and if she was still pissed at me. I had to ask the question, even if it made me an asshole. If we were gonna be together, she'd have to get used to that. Hell, did I even want to be with her? Did she want to be with me, here on Hardtail Ranch?

Thankfully, Cruz's endless questions interrupted that particular train of thought.

"This still don't make sense, man. Why shoot at Aspen, and why now? It's been weeks since they broke up, and Ken's been to the club a few times with a few different women. None of them Aspen. Anyone watching him or her would know that."

As much as I wanted to tell Cruz to shut up, he asked some good goddamn questions. "You saying you think this was all just a diversion?"

Cruz shook his head. "Maybe, yeah, but that doesn't make sense either because now we're all here, just a few feet from Peaches. This Farnsworth dude would definitely know that in advance. It's got to be something else, but I don't know what. Yet."

"I can't find any flaws with that," Wheeler said, sounding half put out he hadn't thought of it. "As a precaution, we should keep everyone in the house, even Martha's evil spawns. No one leaves the ranch until this shit is over, right Gunnar?"

"Fuck yeah." Gunnar rounded the desk and went to the door, pulling it open. "Get what you need, go in groups to make sure the house is covered and then come back in five."

The office emptied out quick enough, leaving me alone with Gunnar. "What's on your mind, Prez?"

He snorted a laugh. "Stop beating yourself up. Aspen is fine. Scared as hell probably, but fine."

"Yeah, no thanks to me."

Peaches knocked on the open door. "Sorry to interrupt the pity party, but I've got some footage you guys might want to see. Or I can come back after you've finished braiding each other's hair?"

Anything but that. "Whatcha got?"

Chapter Twenty-Eight

Aspen

Ever since Peaches said the word lockdown, I was itching to get to the bunkhouse for a few creature comforts. No place had felt like home in a long time. Holden's cabin had started, for the briefest of moments to feel like it, but that failed in the end. He'd made that clear. Still, would a change of clothes and a hairbrush be asking too much?

Of course not. The minute the boys' little powwow down in the front hall was over, I used their departure as a cover to head to the bunkhouse. Alone. It might not have been the smartest move, but I had an errand of my own. I appreciated Holden's help and the help of the Reckless Bastards and even Peaches, but I needed a few damn moments to myself.

Is this what my life had become now, being shot at and protected by bikers? Had my taste in men gotten so poor that my ex was now trying to kill me? That thought pulled a laugh right from the center of my belly, as ridiculous as it was. Ken didn't give a shit about me, certainly not enough to try and take my life.

Then again, my taste had improved only slightly with Holden. Sure, he was a nice guy. A good guy even, but he was also lightning quick to believe the worst about me. It was a shit lesson to learn, that I couldn't outrun or outgrow my past, especially when my fall back plan had been to return home to Vance. Fat chance of that happening now. Daddy would enjoy making sure I knew just how deeply I'd disappointed him.

No, thank you, anything but that.

Was it too much to ask for someone to have had a little bit of faith, of confidence in me?

Pity party for one, please.

No, I needed to have some belief in myself and to stand on my own, to find *my* path in life. That, I vowed, was what would I spend the next few days working on.

While hiding out from a killer.

LOCKED

I crept up to the bunkhouse and slipped inside. As I expected, I found it quiet and dark with all the lights off except for the yellow light from the common room lamp that seemed to shine a spotlight on the fact that Wheeler had brought his stuff back. I briefly wondered why, but I respected his privacy more than I wanted to help. As if I could, anyway. That was when I noticed that it was *too* quiet in the bunkhouse. *Too* dark, too.

There was a weird charge in the air, and just as my instinct to run kicked in, a familiar voice spoke.

"You're not such hot shit. Practically ordinary," she snarled.

I turned, expecting to see a familiar pert nose and freckles that were the only feature not shared by the twins, but it wasn't Evelyn.

"I never claimed to be anything of the sort, Adrian." She was the quiet twin, just as bitchy as Evelyn, but she didn't wield it like a machete, so she flew under the radar. Way under the radar.

"You walk around like you think you're the hottest shit around." The disdain in her voice was evident, but it was the fire burning in her eyes that took me aback. It was hatred.

"I don't think that. The fact that you think so says more about you than it does about me. And you know what? I don't give a damn what you think."

Now was as good a moment as any to start refusing to take any shit from anybody.

"What the hell did Kenny ever see in you anyway?" She gave me an assessing look as she flicked on the floor lamp in the corner, lighting her face almost like the beginning of a terrifying campfire tale. "He says you're boring in bed, you know."

That didn't surprise me at all. "That's what all men say who don't know how to please a woman. Why should I experiment when he can't even satisfy me with normal, vanilla sex?" It didn't surprise me that he'd moved on. Ken was never one to spend too much time on his own. It gave him too much time to think, and to him that was a fate worse than death.

LOCKED

"When the charm wears off, that tiny cock won't be so satisfying. Trust me."

"You take that back, bitch! Kenny is a generous lover. And as soon as I take care of you," she snarled, her eyes wild, crazed as they darted around the room. "When I take care of you, we're gonna live a big life together. The biggest!"

Those were Ken's words if I ever heard them. "Let me guess. In the big city?" I laughed, a sound that was sharp and bitter, even to my own ears. "Yeah he made me that same promise, and a few weeks later we ended up here."

Adrian didn't like the reminder that she wasn't Ken's first. "Yeah, well I'm not like you, a stuck up ice princess not willing to do anything to help out."

Those were definitely Ken's words. I'd heard that speech enough times to recite it in my sleep. "You're right. You aren't like me. I have my own money, which means I never had to participate in his latest scheme, because that's what he is, Adrian, a schemer."

"You're a liar! You're just saying that 'cause you want him back!"

She stood up and scraped her knuckles across one side of her head, looking agitated. Worried.

"Ken is the last thing I want in my life. If you were smart, you'd run in the opposite direction."

"If you were smart you would shut your fuckin' mouth."

A switch flipped inside of her. The wild-eyed Adrian was replaced with a calmer, though just as shaky-handed version. The most noticeable difference was the shaky-handed version now held a gun.

"Kenny was right. You don't know when to shut the hell up."

"You're the perfect little parrot of him," I said. Was this really happening to me twice in one night? "He must be so proud of you, Adrian."

She raised the gun and aimed it at me, and all the blood drained from my face and my hands, leaving me cold with a pounding heart and a deep urge to run.

LOCKED

"Still talking?"

It wasn't smart, but I had a feeling I was dead either way. "Yeah, I am. Because you seem to think Ken is some savior, but he's not. He's broke, owes money to every gaming room and casino from here to Maine. And now some spy owns most of his debt, and that fucker is crazy."

I told her all about my encounter with him, mostly to stall for time, but also if I could save another woman from Ken's clutches, I had to try. Even if she had a nine-millimeter pointed at my head.

She smiled, and it wasn't a happy or satisfied kind of smile. No, it was on the wrong end of the crazy spectrum.

"That's where you'll come in handy," she said.

The hand with the gun motioned for me to head toward my things. I did because she had a gun trained on me.

"So this is a robbery?" It was a novel idea, rob your ex-girlfriend to pay for his next one, but there was a major flaw with it.

"You could say that. Or you could think of it as a donation to true love."

The laugh erupted from me before I could stop it, and yep, it pissed Adrian off. "Sorry. I didn't mean to, it's just…you really love Ken?"

"Don't worry about me and Kenny. Just write down your PIN numbers for your bank and credit cards. Online banking info, too."

She rattled off a long list of items that Ken had probably drilled into her head, and I realized that Adrian was just another pawn, and she was too stupid to realize it.

"He's using you." To be fair, Ken used everyone, but it was all clear now. The reason he kept me around and put up with my refusal to engage in his schemes. I was his escape plan.

"No honey, he's using you. We both are."

LOCKED

"Except Ken's not here, is he? You are, and my guess is you tried to disable the surveillance on the property."

"Shut up!"

I smiled. "You did. So this will all look like his new girlfriend was jealous of the ex and killed her, but not before you give your precious Kenny all of my financial information. You'll be denied bail until trial, and Ken will be spending my money on the next woman."

It was pretty brilliant actually, and if he pulled it off, well I'd be impressed that one of his plans actually worked out.

"You're wrong about most of it. The part where you'll be gone, though, spot on, princess. Now get me those details."

I took my time, digging through my bag even though my wallet was right there. Somewhere behind the lipstick and tampons was the switchblade my daddy gave me on my sixteenth birthday. He'd made the carved wooden handle himself, and I never went anywhere without it. "You know this won't work, don't you?"

Adrian shook her head. "I know that I'd say the same thing in your position."

"Maybe so, but you're not rich, so I wouldn't expect you to understand."

"Really? You do realize I have a gun aimed right at your precious face, don't you?"

"That's not what I meant." She stepped closer, which brought the gun even closer. Though I grew up around guns, had a healthy respect for them. I also had an even healthier fear of the damage they could do to the human body.

"My money is from a trust. That means a certain amount is released to me each month, and I have to sign in person or do a video chat to receive it." One of my granddaddy's fail-safe measures to prevent this very thing from happening.

"You're lying." She wanted that to be the truth, but I was out of reasons to lie, and we both knew it. Adrian poked the gun into my ribs until I winced. It wasn't the perfect moment, but it was the only one I had, so I pulled the knife from my purse and stuck it in her leg before taking off for the front door.

"Stop!" The word came out on an anguished grunt, but the gunshot stopped me.

"Oh, fuck, you shot me!" I fell to the ground in an instant. The bullet had only sliced through a few layers of skin and would require stitches but nothing else, but that didn't stop the searing pain from tearing through my body.

"You fucking shot me!"

"When I say stop, you listen."

"You're one to talk," I grunted from the effort of trying to get my feet under me so I could stand.

"Change of plans. You're coming with me." She waved for me to leave the bunkhouse, using the gun just to make sure I understood the stakes.

"Don't be stupid. This can't possibly work." But Adrian was beyond listening, using the gun to push me out of the bunkhouse.

"The car is...oh, shit."

Oh, shit was right. Gunnar, Holden, and Wheeler all stood in front of us, three big ass guns aimed our way.

Chapter Twenty-Nine

Holden

"See that sliver right there? It's part of a car, some type of sedan."

Peaches pointed to a dark triangle, and suddenly the form appeared. "This is the small camera on the Hardtail Ranch arch as you enter the property."

"You said that already," I told her. It was the tenth time we looked at the footage, and even Gunnar had bowed out five views ago. Nothing new had popped out. Yet. The car looked like a basic, dark-colored sedan. From the angle, it was a late, four door model, maybe a luxury brand. "Nothing on the model or the plates?"

One brow arched at the question I'd asked no less than a dozen times.

"Nope. I'll need to update the surveillance out there so this doesn't happen again." Her tone was deadly serious and guilt-filled.

"Don't take on this asshole's guilt, Peaches." Those fiery hazel eyes flashed gratitude before turning back to the screen.

"Thanks," she whispered so low I wasn't entirely sure she'd said anything at all.

"Okay, now look here." She pointed at the screen, and the third angle appeared, the one right in front of the fences where I let the horses enjoy the warm days.

"Did you see it?"

"Yeah, but not clearly. Run it again." This time I saw what my tired, anxious eyes had missed before.

"It's a shoe. A goddamn shoe." One of those fancy leather shoes that were a mix between a dress shoe and a casual one. "I'd know that brown leather anywhere."

"You do? How?" Peaches' interest was piqued, despite the circumstances.

"Aspen threw them at Ken at The Barn Door the night she caught him fucking someone else. Barely missed my head by an inch." Even that seemed a lifetime ago.

LOCKED

"So it is Ken? That son of a bitch." Peaches growled his name. I joined her as one shot sounded. Close. "What the fuck?"

"Gunshots. Get low and stay here," I whispered. "Gunnar?"

"Headed towards the bunkhouse," she said.

That was all I needed to hear to pull my piece out and jog down the stairs, ready to join him. If that fucker was still here on the property, I'd make sure he'd regret it.

I hadn't seen Aspen since we left the storage shed, and that was over an hour ago. She hadn't appeared in the kitchen for coffee and Martha's delicious coffee cake, and she wasn't watching TV with Maisie and Martha in the living room. Suddenly that shot made a lot more sense, and my feet moved even faster until I was the first one to arrive at the bunkhouse.

The door smacked open, and I was met with the most welcome sight, Aspen's face. But it wasn't twisted in anger or beaming with love. Her skin was pale, and her expression was fear or worry as she walked at an odd pace, stiff. Wooden.

"Don't be stupid, Adrian." Her gaze darted behind her, and I knew what she was saying.

Adrian. One of Martha's evil spawn. "The car is…oh shit."

"Oh shit is right, little girl."

She gasped and peeked over Aspen's shoulder with a lopsided smile and an erratic gaze. "Holden, Kenny was hoping you'd show up."

"Bet he didn't expect me to bring backup, did he?" The man was a coward. Who knew what he had in store for Aspen? "I can't believe you're doing his dirty work, though."

She shrugged. "None of you guys were ever gonna notice me anyway, and she won't need any money when she's dead."

Aspen winced and arched her back as the gun dug into her flesh. "Now back up or I'll shoot her right here."

"You do that, and you're dead. No one gets the money, and Ken runs off with, what was that chick's name, Aspen?"

"Paige," she bit out, glaring at me like she wanted to shoot me herself.

"That's right, Paige will get Ken, and you will be dead." She didn't seem to be moved by my words at all. "Look around, Adrian, there's no way out of this for you."

"Wrong again, cowboy. You out there, baby?"

I didn't have to turn to know that half the Reckless Bastards now had their backs to the bunkhouse and to me, facing the land beyond.

"Two o'clock!" Aspen's words were cut off by a cry of pain caused by Adrian sticking her finger into a bloody wound on her arm. "Ouch!"

Ken stepped out from the shadows, looking like the piece of shit scumbag he was in khaki pants and a peach golf shirt.

"I'm here, honey." He waved his gun around like that shit was supposed to scare us. "Looks like Aspen is causing more trouble than she's worth. Again."

"Looks like you've bitten off more than you can chew. Again. Asshole." That was my girl, deep in shit and unafraid to keep going for the jugular. I hoped it worked to her advantage for the next ten minutes.

"These bikers are no concern of mine. They have bigger, badder enemies than me. And if you give me what I want, we'll get out of here so they can focus on their real problems." Ken turned to me. "What do you say?"

Too much was happening, too much unspoken shit was being said, and I couldn't focus on it all. Not and keep Aspen safe while trying to figure out what Ken was trying really hard not to say. "I say fuck you, Ken."

He laughed. "Don't stay for the money. The bitch is as cheap as she is frigid."

It took every ounce of willpower I possessed not to charge the asshole and beat him to a pulp. "It helps when you feed her a steady diet of ten-inch cock." A few of the guys laughed, but I knew they would.

"Bullshit."

"It's true," Cruz added with a laugh. "We all call him Mah-Dick. I would've chosen anaconda, but it was already taken."

"Shut the fuck up!" Ken frazzled was about as intimidating as a spinster aunt, but he was reckless and armed, which made him a clear threat. "I just want the cash I'm owed. I paid for everything."

He bitched and whined about money while I played his words in my head.

"Shit. Wheeler you were right, get to the house!" I hoped my words carried over Ken's pitiful insistence that Aspen owed him something.

I heard footsteps behind me, and I knew one set belonged to Gunnar, who took off to save his family. Cruz and Slayer were still with me, one gun trained on Ken and the other on Adrian. "I guess you aren't just a dumb biker after all."

"And I guess you really are a dumb fuck." The safety was on his gun, and I charged, closing the distance between us as fast as I could.

"No!" Adrian's voice rang out and then a gunshot. Then came the white-hot pain that brought me to my knees. I couldn't move as warm blood pumped out of my body. All I could do was watch those expensive brown shoes move back and forth in small shuffles while two more shots rang out, and the tips of those shoes went skyward.

"Aspen." The word barely made it out of my mouth before darkness began to claim me. My last thought, my last hope was that none of those bullets had marred Aspen's perfect skin.

Chapter Thirty

Aspen

"Why the hell isn't he awake yet, Dr. Keyes?" Twenty-four full hours had passed since that psycho bitch shot Holden in the back, and I hadn't seen those beautiful blue eyes since.

She put her hands on my shoulders, staring right at me. "I sedated him. The pain is terrible right now, and the best thing for his body is rest."

My shoulders sank. "Oh. That sounds right. Sorry, Dr. Keyes."

"No worries, and please, call me Annabelle." She stood beside me in the same guestroom where I'd recuperated, staring out at the ranch and put another hand to my shoulder.

"He's going to be okay, Aspen. It'll take a while, but he'll recover."

I knew that, but how would he recover? "Will he be able to walk? He hit his head pretty hard. What if he can't see?" What if all those things everyone said about me was true? What if I didn't have what it took to take care of him in a compromised position?

"Shit, Annabelle."

She let out a huff-laugh that held no amusement and just a hint of commiseration. "You'll take it day by day because that's all you can do, Aspen."

"What if I can't do even that? What if I'm as useless as everyone says I am?" Why the hell was I spilling my guts to a stranger? I had no idea. But I had to talk to someone, and she was here.

"The fact that you're even worried about him means you're more than up to the job. I suspect your heart has a huge stake in his recovery."

I nodded. "I do love him. But we're doomed. I just want to make sure he gets better, and then I'll be on my way."

"The hell you will."

LOCKED

I gasped and turned to the bed. "Holden! You're awake." I was at his side, hands pressed to his face and lips smashed to his. "My God, you're awake!"

His lips curled into a tight grin. "All I had to do was get shot to make you forgive me?"

"Who says I've forgiven you?" He grinned and his hand gripped my arm tighter.

"Hurts like hell," he grunted out. "What happened?"

The last thing I wanted to do was relive those fifteen seconds that took about five years off my life. Everything slowed down as he charged Ken with a determined and decidedly murderous expression on his face. Before I knew what was happening, Adrian slammed me to the ground and raised her gun at Holden's back.

"You went down, and Slayer put one between Adrian's eyes. Someone else, not Cruz, killed Ken. You'll have to get the details from Gunnar."

Annabelle chose that moment to step between us. "Let me check him out, and then you two can talk."

With a nod, I left and paced up and down the length of the hall, unwilling to stray too far away from Holden. He'd been shot, trying to protect me, and I couldn't forget that. No one had ever made such a sacrifice for me, and I needed him to know that I recognized his sacrifice and appreciated it. I wanted to tell him that I loved him even though it probably wouldn't matter.

"Okay. Now go have your talk." Annabelle wrapped me in a hug and walked away, her soft footfalls barely audible on the hardwood steps.

I pushed open the door and found Holden's gaze fixed on the door. "You really plan to leave once I'm all healed up?"

I nodded. "I think it's for the best, Holden. I really do." I took the small space beside him on the bed and held one of his big hands in both of mine. "Meeting you again Holden has been an eye-opener. Seeing myself

LOCKED

through your eyes, good and bad, then and now, has forced me to own up to some hard truths about myself."

"I hope you weren't too hard on yourself because I kind of like the girl you are today."

I wished that were true. "I just want to say thank you. I appreciate everything you did for me. For my body. Even for my heart."

God knows, he touched my heart in ways I didn't think possible, and I would be forever grateful to him for it.

"And instead of staying to see what we could be, you're running away?"

"Not until you're better." It wasn't like I wanted to leave. "We both know the question is do I leave now or later, once we've burned out and hate each other."

"Or maybe our star will burn bright until we're too old to look directly at the sun anymore. You ever think of that?"

Only about a bazillion times. "How could we possibly?"

I didn't want to hear the answer, so I stood and started to pace. "I need to tell you something, but only so you understand."

"I'm listening." His voice was calm and cool, but his gaze was intense, catching every detail, so I held myself still and spoke.

"I love you, Holden. Okay? I love you enough to see that we'll never work. You'll always see me as that cruel girl who stomped on your heart, and I'll spend the rest of my life trying to prove I'm not her. It'll exhaust us both until we hate each other."

"So you're leaving me, for me?" He chuckled.

"Holden, don't."

"No, Aspen, dammit. *You* don't! I love you, too. And now you're telling me that you're leaving and it's what's best for me. I call bullshit."

"Excuse me?"

"You heard me, sweetheart. Bullshit. You're a coward."

"I am not! It's called being practical. You should try it sometime!" I huffed. "See? You just barely woke up, and we're already fighting."

"We're not fighting. We're discussing." His tone changed, and I froze, feet rooted to the spot and unable to move. "And I understand. You're too afraid to give us a chance. No biggie."

I knew I was being baited, knew it down to my toes, but still, a big part of me wanted to stay and prove to Holden and to myself that I had what it took to stay. "I'm not afraid of anything. Except guns."

"And love." Holden reached out a hand to me. "What do you say, Aspen? Want to do something really fucking terrifying?"

"You mean like be together?"

He nodded, and a smile stretched across his face. "Yep. Have a few babies, maybe get married. Tend to the ranch. Sounds like fun to me."

"Horse poop," I added, feeling more excited by the future he painted by the day.

He rolled his eyes. "Lots of horse poop. And holiday parties. Good food, booze."

"Sounds awful," I sighed. "Really scary." It sounded like my very own version of heaven on earth.

"Right? But I think together, it might be a little less terrifying."

I smiled and kissed his lips. "You might be right, Holden."

"So you'll stay with me, and we can get started on forever?"

The hope and eagerness in his voice was enough to unravel my resolve. I melted against his side. "I will," I said hesitantly. "We can." This time with more resolve.

"Good, 'cause I'm too damn weak to chain you to the bed."

I laughed and smacked another kiss to his sweet mouth. "I love you, Holden."

"Sweet, sweet, Aspen. I love you too."

LOCKED

Now those words were music to my ears.

KB WINTERS

LOCKED

Epilogue

Holden ~ a few weeks later

"What the hell do you mean it was Farnsworth?" A few weeks after I'd been shot, I finally had a few minutes alone with Gunnar to find out what the fuck happened that day.

Gunnar shrugged and sat down at my kitchen table. "Cruz never even got a chance to fire his gun, but there was one in the middle of Ken's forehead. It wasn't any of us. Plus, there was a note."

He pulled a sheet of paper from the inside of his jacket and slid it across the table.

I unfolded the heavy paper and read the message. "Sweet Peaches, this wasn't a favor to you. I clean up my own messes. Always do. Farnsworth." I looked up at Gunnar. "That's it?"

"Wasn't it enough? If not for your quick thinking, who knows what might have happened. This letter was on the porch by the time Wheeler got there. He was close, Holden. Too fucking close."

"If he wanted her dead, she would be. What's Peaches think about the letter?"

"Fuck if I know. She's kind of folded in on herself. Barely talks to anyone other than Annabelle and Hazel. She wants to go back east to look through some of her shit, figure out what this Farnsworth wants with her."

I could tell by the set of his shoulders, the dark scowl on his face, what he thought of that idea.

"Go with her, and I'll move to the big house to help out with Maisie. Hell, I'm useless on the ranch. At least we might get ahead of this asshole. Doc Annabelle says I have at least another month of lying around and taking it easy."

"You'd do that?"

"Fuck yeah, why not? That kid's cute as hell and maybe a week or so with her will help me convince Aspen that we're ready." It was too soon, and I knew that, but I was sure. Soon she would be too.

LOCKED

"I won't argue with you, then. I'll get Ford and the others to move your shit since you can't do it, old man."

I flipped him off. "I won't turn down the help, but you're older than me, grandpa."

Gunnar laughed and flipped me off on his way to the fridge. "These days, I feel old as fuck. Maisie is getting bigger, and it's getting harder to hide this shit from her."

Plus the little girl was too damn smart for her own good. She missed very little and quickly picked up on emotions, which was tricky on a ranch filled with former military men.

"My ma never hid shit from me, if that helps."

He grunted. "It doesn't, but thanks anyway."

"Sure." There was another issue, one he hadn't mentioned, but I knew had to weigh heavy on him. "What do you plan to do about Martha?"

"Fuck if I know. Peaches says to talk to her, see what she wants to do, but I can't keep her on, can I?"

"Worried she might seek her revenge where you're vulnerable?"

He glared at me. "I wasn't until now."

"Peaches is right. Talk to Martha first. Evelyn too." The last thing we needed was two pissed off women with access to the President's house and family. And food.

"I was hoping you had a better alternative. This is the last thing I need, and don't get me started on Farnsworth."

"Hard to get started on a nondescript guy with the same name as a bunch of other dead G-men. If anyone can figure it out, it's your woman."

"Yeah, she's pretty great, right?" Gunnar shook his head. "But she's vulnerable here and doesn't realize it."

"That's what we're here for. Let the women and the babies live their lives without knowing what that safety costs, right?"

LOCKED

"Yeah, but dammit. No woman is more stubborn than Peaches." He was right about that, which made her hard to protect.

"That's why she has you. To keep her in line. Just don't tell her I said so."

Gunnar doubled over with laughter, nearly dropping two bottles of beer fresh from the fridge.

"You're far too valuable for me to share that." He blew out a breath and sighed. "Here's to a few fucking moments of peace, man."

We knocked our bottles together and took several long, slow pulls. A few fucking moments of peace sounded nice.

Really fucking nice.

* * * *

~ THE END ~

Acknowledgements

Thank you so much for making my books a success! I appreciate all of you! Thanks to all of my beta readers, street teamers, ARC readers and Facebook fans. Y'all are THE BEST!

And a huge very special thanks to Jessie! I'm such a *hot mess, but without your keen sense of organization and skills, I'd be a burny fiery inferno of hot mess!! Thank you!

And a very special thanks to my editors (who sometimes have to work all through the night! *See HOT MESS above!) Thank you for making my words make sense.

Copyright © 2019 KB Winters and BookBoyfriends Publishing LLC

KB WINTERS

About The Author

KB Winters is a Wall Street Journal and USA Today Bestselling Author of steamy hot books about Bikers, Billionaires, Bad Boys and Badass Military Men. Just the way you like them. She has an addiction to caffeine, tattoos and hard-bodied alpha males. The men in her books are very sexy, protective and sometimes bossy, her ladies are...well...*bossier*!

Living in sunny Southern California, with her five kids and three fur babies, this embarrassingly hopeless romantic writes every chance she gets!

You can reach me at Facebook.com/kbwintersauthor and at kbwintersauthor@gmail.com

Copyright © 2019 KB Winters and BookBoyfriends Publishing LLC

Printed in Great Britain
by Amazon